ALSO BY JOSEPH COLWELL

FROM LICHEN ROCK PRESS

NATURE ESSAY COLLECTIONS

Canyon Breezes: Exploring Magical Places in Nature

Zephyr of Time: Meditations on Time and Nature

Echoes of Time: Reflections on the Mesas and Canyons of the Dominguez-Escalante National Conservation Area

FICTION

Tales of Ravens Nest: A Life, A Place: Stories and Reflections

MEMOIR

Tuscola: A Memoir
Place, Time, and Meanings of a Hometown

FROM PAGE PUBLISHING

FICTION

Sands of Time: A Flight of Discovery and Search for Meanings of Time

THE HERMIT
OF PUCCINI RIDGE

A Story of a Life

JOSEPH COLWELL

Lichen Rock Press
Hotchkiss, Colorado 81419

Early versions of "Of Brambles and Old Fences" and "The Root Cellar" were published in *Zephyr of Time,* 2016.

Editing and photography: Katherine Colwell
Design and publishing services: Constance King Design

Lichen Rock Press
Hotchkiss, Colorado
ColwellCedars.com

ISBN: 978-0-996-2222-5-9
Printed in USA

Author's Note

In the creative minds of writers, fiction is invented and not necessarily true. But usually there is at least a grain of truth, based on some experience or knowledge of the writer. Speaking through the voice of Jake, I searched for the truth, then continued with my imagination where facts and experiences merged into mists of the past.

~ Joseph Colwell, April 2022

Contents

Editor's Introduction

I was privileged to edit the novella and short story collection written by Jake Collins titled, "Tales of Ravens Nest." After Jake passed, my wife Tori and I had discovered the previously unknown writings in Jake's extensive files, with instructions for publishing. Since then, further delving into his files brought to light more writings, which I am also honored to edit and publish. The following is Jake's preface to his manuscript "The Hermit of Puccini Ridge."

~ Alistaire Corey

Jake's Preface

Dear Reader,

Relax and sit back. Let me tell you two stories. They are stories I felt compelled to write for two reasons. First, I needed to research and understand how a person could live amongst the beauty I find in this place and treat it like a garbage dump. What was the story of this person and what happened to her that affected her life? The second reason was personal. In my research into this person and her life, my attitudes changed over time, but I still felt both angry and sad. The spirit of this person hovered over me until I could totally erase her impact on the land. Writing this was as much healing me as the land itself.

The story of Opal is based on sketchy facts, but the truth is now hidden in the passing clouds of time, buried with the lives of those who lived it. There is no one left alive who knows the complete story. It is complicated and sad, although with a few strands of light and hope interwoven in the tale. It is about one person's struggle to live with despair and start anew. It is about beauty hidden beneath the trash we strew around us. Our task, in the story and in life, is to seek that beauty and let it erase the trash.

This story as told is fiction. I originally intended it to be a historical novel but I could not find enough facts to do this. Names are changed. Characters are based on real people, places are real places. It is not important to know their real names.

I never met the actual person I call Opal. I have not even seen a photograph of her. She was dead before my wife and I came to own what was once her property. But she did exist. This place became her solace if you could call it that. She survived here, belonging to something comforting to her. For over fifty years it was her home, her property, where she lived in seclusion.

We purchased the land from the speculator who bought it from her heirs, and I can trace 'ownership' from the Utes (and their ancestors of a dozen millennia), to the federal government, to Opal who acquired it through the Homestead Act. Of the few 'post-Ute-removal' owners who claimed this land, only she became part of the land. Her spirit still roams the sky above, but that is part of the story. The land was untamed and wild, keeping the freedom of everything that had passed this way for millennia.

After we built our home on 'Bean Ridge' and moved here full time, I researched Opal's story. I talked to the old-timers and neighbors who may have known her. Most reactions were along the lines of "I can't help you. We didn't know Opal."

I also found out a lot about the area I call Bean Ridge. People who lived in this area, even as late as the 1960s, found it a challenging place to live. Lack of good roads, difficult access to schools, and inadequate irrigation water, all left these people independent, but also reliant on each other. Even today, people who live here like the semi-remoteness and isolation. Opal lived through a time where her world changed significantly—for those who interacted with that outside world. She did not.

I discovered a few interesting stories and realized that in order to write her story I would have to make most of it up. As they say in the movies, 'based on a true story.' There are threads of truth, but most of the details are inventions. I changed most names, but the locations and some of the people are real. Those who shared stories with me knew her as a legend. A legend often creates myths. As with all legends, we will never know what really happened and what did not. There is a saying "when the legend becomes fact, print the legend." This is the legend.

For our first few years here, Opal and her impact affected me. Her decaying log cabin was still standing, home to pack rats and weasels. Tangles of fences crisscrossed the quarter-square mile. Hillsides covered with rusted cans, bottles, wire, car parts, and other junk gave me endless days of work to clean up. Very little was worth saving. Countless trips to the landfill slowly erased the negative and unsightly impacts of Opal's life here. I excavated her root cellar, tore down and burned her cabin, tore out the fences, tore down outhouses and sheds. Slowly I put our own stamp on the property. I sprayed weeds. I planted flowers and trees. I built new buildings and made it into a place of natural beauty which it was before she cast her neglect over it. I spent years clearing tangles of dead juniper and sumac from the creek bottoms and hillsides. I built trails, improved wildlife habitat, reduced the fire danger. As I write this, Ravens Nest bears few traces of the Opal years. As all spirits do, Opal has retreated over time and dissipated in the west wind. Her memory now floats as gently as the cattail seeds blowing in November breezes.

The second 'story' I tell is my own—a collection of reflections over time. For a while, I glorified Opal and her spirit. Then I cursed her filth and mistreatment of a sacred place. The journey I took in learning—then writing—about Opal also needed telling, as a way of my own healing. The dark cloud that Opal spread on this land needed cleansing. Now, Opal is an almost-forgotten memory, just as the Ute who crossed the mesa for untold centuries, leaving nothing but an occasional chip of flint. Just as I don't want them forgotten, I can't forget Opal either. She was a part of this, just as someday, I will be a similarly forgotten part of history. Opal is an enigma, a mystery who likely cringes at my attempt to learn about her; she would not have read this story. She suffered mental problems that I am not qualified to judge or even understand and that is part of the story.

I wrote my reflections as I came to know this place. It is also how I came to try and understand Opal and her life. The reflections occur over twenty years and changed as I learned the few facts I found. After you read both Opal's story and my own journey, let the breezes blow away the sadness and fill you with the beauty that surrounds us all, if only we look deep enough for it.

The breezes are the only constant here. Opal's story and my reflections are a brief blink of an eye. Standing on the end of the mesa, a few hundred feet from her cabin site, we look over the valley and the river, seeing the distant mountains of snow-capped peaks. Even those are not constant since it was several blinks of the geologic eye when they were cauldrons of boiling lava and spewing ash from volcanoes that formed the San Juan Mountains. They and the rocks beneath my feet—stretching miles within the Earth—have witnessed far more than the Opals and Willys of this world. We are all newcomers and the pain and isolation all have felt are no more than a passing breeze or falling snowflake. Each of us leaves a legacy—or a legend—soon to be forgotten.

~ Jake Collins

Part I

OPAL'S STORY

One

OPAL WAS JOLTED AWAKE—not by the train jerking to a stop—but by the conductor walking down the aisle calling "Dawson, Colorado. We stop for ten minutes then move east towards Gunnison and Denver. First call for Dawson, folks. Welcome to the Rocky Mountains."

She was dog-tired after having to change trains three times during the long journey over mountains and across deserts from California. She was home now. "For good," Opal sighed to herself. She did not have wonderful memories of her childhood here, but it was still home. She grew up with these mountains ringing the valley. There were not many people here, especially compared to her stay in California. She had learned to live in the city, and had made progress in feeling comfortable with being around people and with surviving on her own. But then things went terribly wrong. She looked forward to being home in Colorado and away from California.

As she walked into the train station, she spotted her mother Della waiting to greet her—smiling yet shaking her head slowly. She embraced Opal in a motherly hug and Opal burst into tears.

She had been gone only four years, but those years had been turbulent. Leaving Colorado in the fall of 1926, the young rambunctious Opal of almost twenty was ready to challenge the world. She was a newlywed, accompanying her new husband westward to the golden coast of the California he bragged about. She knew at the time her mother's disapproval of marrying this stranger. She did it anyway, partly as her way of announcing her independence.

As she dried her eyes and gathered her three bags—her worldly possessions—Opal didn't think of Paul at all. If she did, she would unleash the venom that could poison her even more than Paul Koenig had poisoned her, both mentally and physically. She looked back at the train as it left the station, continuing its eastward journey heading into the wall of mountains. She vowed she would never leave these mountains—her home—ever again.

They walked out the front door of the small station, a remnant of the optimism of the fading pioneer days of a few decades past. Della blinked in the bright sun, then looked around for Thad, her second husband and father of three of her six children. Opal's father Whitney had abandoned Della, Opal, and her brother Preston and sister Ruth, years ago, setting the stage for Opal's distrust of men. Her father as far as Opal knew was in California now, but she'd had no inclination to look for him while she was there.

"There he is," Della waved as she saw the beat-up truck pull into the empty field next to the building. The bed was full of feed sacks, which Thad had picked up while Della waited for the train to arrive, only an hour behind schedule.

"He looks older," Opal said softly to Della as she walked to the passenger side. Stretching over the side, she tucked her suitcases behind the sacks of feed.

"Opal, honey, he is older and so are you." She gently pushed Opal in the front seat next to Thad. It was a tight squeeze for the three of them. Thad gave Opal a perfunctory kiss on the cheek as he looked her over. "Good to see you Opal, but you look worn out. Long train ride, huh?"

"Let's just go home. I'm tired and I don't want to talk about any of it. Not much room in here. I can sit in the back."

"Nonsense," chided Della as she shifted her ample rear to make more room. Opal rested her head on the back window and closed her eyes, oblivious to the discomfort in the crowded seat. Thad looked at Opal, then smiled as he looked at Della. "Welcome home. Guess nothing has changed much has it?"

"Now Thad, don't pick a fight," Della pleaded as she looked at Opal, pushing a strand of hair out of her face. Opal didn't open her eyes. She was asleep by the time they left the edge of Dawson. The drive was a long one to Beaver Creek over a winding and rutted dirt road.

~

As the sun was setting, Thad pulled into the yard of their small home in Wolf Park north of town. When he honked to move the goats out of the way, Opal jerked awake. Della patted Opal's hand as she opened the door to get out. "We're home, Opal. You're welcome here as long as you want. With Preston gone now, the north bedroom can be yours. Eugene and Rand share the east bedroom; Dinah is in the upstairs room." Opal almost fell out the door. She grabbed two of her suitcases and stumbled through the front door, which Thad was holding open for her. Della looked at Thad as she carried in the third suitcase.

"Della, I'll put the feed in the barn. Looks like you may have your hands full with that crazy daughter of yours. I'll try and stay out of your way. Call when supper is ready." Thad went to the truck to unload his supplies.

After putting her suitcases in her room, Opal went in the kitchen, grabbed a bottle of goat milk and a slab of bread, returned to the bedroom, closed the door, and didn't come out again until morning. No one heard her sobs that night as she muffled her face in a soft down pillow. She needed to be alone. She was thankful she didn't have to share the room with her half-sister Dinah.

Della and Thad waited until Eugene, Rand and Dinah had gone to bed, then sat at the kitchen table to discuss Opal's situation. Thad had not been around Opal that much. When he met and married Della, Opal was already out of the house, living with her older sister Ruth and her husband and small children near Beaver Creek. He had never felt at ease with Opal, and Opal hadn't seemed to feel at ease with anyone. Now that she'd returned, she seemed even more aloof and distant. Opal left Colorado an attractive carefree young woman; she returned home looking much older, less attractive, and withdrawn. Thad sensed a deep anger, and wanted to give Opal time to adjust to a new life back in Colorado.

Della reassured Thad that Opal was just tired from the long train ride. After Opal's bad marriage, Della felt confident Opal would cheer up in a few days, or at most, weeks, of rest. She started to say that getting back with old friends would also help, but she realized that Opal had few friends here.

For the next week, Opal did come out of her room and eat meals with Thad, Della, and the rest of the family but didn't speak much. When she did, she asked questions about her brothers and sisters. Della thought this strange, since other than Ruth, Opal never did spend much time either playing with or being close to her siblings. Opal was a loner as a child and fought with those who were close to her age. Since Opal was one of the older children, she complained about having to do chores while Della was either having children or raising them.

Now living with her mother and step-father, and sharing the house with half-brothers and half-sister, Opal helped care for them, although they were old enough they didn't need much attention. She felt she had nothing in common with them other than living in the same house. They could sense she was uncomfortable around them so they kept their distance as much as they could.

One day, while Opal was sitting on the back porch bench peeling potatoes for dinner, Thad came in from working in the barn. He sat in the cane rocker and fanned his face with his sweat-stained felt hat. "Opal, you been here, what, four months now? What are your plans? We like having you here, but this ain't natural, just sittin' around like this. Somethin's botherin' you, huh?"

She didn't look up when she spoke in a very soft voice. "You don't want me here, I will look for something else."

"Damn it, Opal," Thad stood up, turned around, then sat next to Opal on the bench. "I didn't say that. I'd just like to have a talk with you, but you always find something else to do whenever I try to speak to you. I worry about you. Della is fretting about you. Haven't you talked to her either?"

"We talk," Opal muttered as she picked up another potato.

"You're, what? Twenty-three? You don't want to be with another man, that's okay with me. What I heard, that Koenig fella was no good, and I'd guess he probably mistreated you. You don't want to share that, that's all right. None of my business. But damned tarnation, it ain't good for you to shut yourself out like this. We can try and find you a job. The packing sheds always need help. I know there are rich folks in Dawson that could use help in cleaning and helping with their kids. Maybe even teaching. Della says you were good at math when you put your mind to it."

Thad pulled a stalk of tall grass growing by the porch and started picking his teeth with it. Opal continued to peel potatoes, never once looking up at Thad.

"He beat me. He forced himself on me. He was no good at all. I'm glad he's dead." She unbuttoned the bottom buttons on her blouse and exposed her stomach. A long scar ran from beneath her waist to nearly her breasts. She wasn't wearing a brassiere. Her left breast had a scar below the nipple.

"See that?" She held her left breast. "He did that. I was sick when he came home drunk one night and he cut me with a knife. I'd have killed him myself 'cept he did it first. Got in a knife fight in Singapore or Hong Kong or somewhere in Asia. Police fished his body out of the bay, cut up so bad, they couldn't identify it until his shipmates reported him missing. Bastard deserved to die a miserable stinking death. I hope he suffered."

Thad started to reach over to console Opal, but he stopped. There were no tears in her eyes. Just a glare that scared Thad with its hatred.

"I had no idea, Opal. I'm sorry." Thad took off his hat and ran his finger around the brim. He stood up and spit out the grass. "No one should be treated like that. Inhuman. I'd'a' killed him myself if I'd known. You better believe it. I would have."

Opal slowly buttoned her blouse. She continued to peel one potato after another.

Thad paced back and forth. "Does Della know this?"

"Not the details. Tell her. I don't care."

"We can arrange for you to talk with somebody. Doctor, maybe. Preacher? There's people you can talk with."

"Talking ain't doin' me no good. Talkin' didn't do this to me. Bastard Paul did. Can't talk to him anymore, can I?"

"Damn it, you should be busy doin somethin'. Just ain't good to sit around like this. Gives you too much time to think about things, time to let that hatred fester, and infect your brain."

"I'm better off by myself. One man treated me bad. He's dead. One man treated me good. He's dead too—because of me. Just find me a place somewhere by myself. I can raise a few pigs, cows. I don't need a man. Not anymore, never." She wiped her eyes, although Thad saw no sign of tears. He didn't understand why she could relate this story so calmly. That was what concerned him—it wasn't natural.

Opal finished the last potato and stood up, brushing off her skirt. Thad looked at her carefully. Opal was still an attractive woman, if you could get past the tattered clothes, the uncombed hair, and the lines of misery drawn across her face. She could be good-looking and find a good man. Thad knew some man could restore Opal's trust. This hatred was poison, he thought. And Opal knew it. How could he help make her care about life again?

Thad stood there for several minutes after Opal disappeared through the screen door. He thought about what she said: one man treated her good. Who was that? She wasn't talking about him. He was surprised she opened up as much as she did. Two dead men. One must be her husband. He would ask Della about the other one.

Thad and Della took a walk after supper. The cottonwoods were brilliant yellow and the wild purple asters were fading in the autumn coolness. A breeze was coming down off the mesa.

"I think this might be a tough winter," Thad said, mostly for something to say.

Della looked up at Sheep Mountain, lightly dusted with snow from two nights before. She brushed a strand of hair out of her face. She looked at Thad, then at the ground. She reached down, picked one aster out of a large clump, and shook off an iridescent green bee.

"Opal talked to you this afternoon didn't she?"

"That girl still bothers me. She actually opened up for a minute or two, but then slammed the door back shut. Somethin' wrong with Opal." He stopped and looked at Della.

"I knew about the scar. She told me about that a while back. I was afraid to tell you," Della said softly. "He knifed her, but the big scar was from the operation. She can't never have kids. They took out her womanhood. He gave her some bad diseases."

"Is she okay now?"

"Far as I can tell. Physically anyway. She's still a tight-lipped girl. That's what bothers me, what it did, or is doing to her mind."

"Opal mentioned something about one man who treated her right. What was that supposed to mean?"

Della twirled the aster as she spoke. She didn't look at Thad but seemed to be talking to the mountains as much as to him. "Opal tells things when they are ripe and ready to come out. Try to pull something out of her and you get silence. I've gotten a lot of silence since she got back. Far as I know, which ain't much, she was foolin' around with a man. Don't know if he was married or not, but he was nice to her. I can't blame her for messing with him since her husband was such a no account. He died somehow, but I don't know much more than that. She said something vague that gives me the feeling he was murdered, but I just don't know."

"Well I'm real sorry bad things happened to her, but bad things happen to a lot of people. Look at how Whitney treated you." Thad rarely mentioned the name of Della's first husband, but whenever he did, he mumbled under his breath, that worthless SOB. "She needs to get over it and on with her life. She said she didn't want a man. She can't make a living here in this valley. No jobs. And as a single woman?"

Thad knelt down and picked up a clod of dirt. He squeezed it in his hands, dropped it and wiped his hands on his overalls. "Still good soil moisture. That's good—heading into winter." He pulled up a wheatgrass stalk and put it in his mouth; Thad was a natural rancher, appreciating the taste of grass seeping into his mouth.

"She has been a help to me with Eugene and Rand and Dinah, but she still spends a lot of time alone," Della said. "I've been asking around. Cousin Tater up on Bean Ridge says there is still some government land available to homestead up there. Not good for much, but it's on the edge of the mesa, where it drops off to Rock Mesa. If she wants to be off by herself, maybe she could go up there."

"My God, Della, she couldn't make a living up there. We'd still have to support her." Thad picked his teeth with the grass stalk. It broke off between his front teeth. "Damn, hate it when it gets stuck in there."

He reached into his shirt pocket, pulled out a small pocket knife and flipped it open. He carefully worked the blade tip between his teeth, pulling out the piece of grass. "We work hard enough to support ourselves. We can't provide for her as well. Opal is still an attractive young woman, although she has certainly let herself go the past few months. She needs to socialize more."

Della shook her head. "Something has changed her. She always was an independent child. I'm not sure she would fit in anywhere. I hope this is just temporary and she gets her head attached. But I have this feeling something snapped in her head and she won't fit in with normal people. I just don't know." Della trailed off, then looked at Thad.

"Tater says he gets good cream money off his cows. Opal could raise a cow or two and maybe some goats and chickens. It might be worth a try. It's an eighty-acre piece with a little grass. Even some water in a creek." Della looked at the sky, then back to Thad. "We got to do something. You are right about that. I don't know what else to do."

Thad watched a pair of mallards fly over, headed for the river. "Yeah.

Something. Maybe I'll go up and see Tater tomorrow." He shook his head as they turned and walked back to the house. Della reached over and held his hand as they walked. He couldn't remember the last time she had done that.

Two

Tater drove his battered black pickup—speckled with rust and splattered with red mud—down the track through sagebrush to the edge of a rocky pasture. Someone had done a not very thorough job of removing rocks and brush from the field to the west of the track; they had attempted to divert irrigation water into the field, but the water was too little to do much good. Irrigation up here on Bean Ridge was in its infancy, with not near enough to go 'round. Earlier attempts to turn the mesa into apple orchards had failed miserably—rainy years a decade ago helped trees get established, now half of them stood stark and dead from lack of season-long water. Yearly precipitation was less than fourteen inches, with little coming in June and July when it was needed most.

He stopped the pickup where the track—still gently going downhill—faded to a deer trail. The mesa itself continued its drop to Rock Mesa five hundred feet below. Thad was the first to get out of the truck. Tater sat in the seat while Thad walked around the front of the truck. He ran his hand along the hood, knocking off a clump of mud caked on the grill.

"This is it, huh?" he drawled as he kicked a dried-up cow pie.

Tater opened his door and got out. "Yeah. Eighty acres of rock and sagebrush. And juniper and pinyon. Little bit of grass. Lots of sky," he said as he looked off to the south. Early winter snow on the distant San Juan Mountains gleamed white in the haze.

"Are the boundaries marked?" Thad asked.

"I saw a boundary tree down on the creek. No other survey markers I could find. I'm pretty sure this pile of rocks is the north line. Whoever applies for homestead will have to get it surveyed, but I'm sure the gov'ment will do it proper."

"Not good for a hell of a lot is it?" Thad said as he picked a stem of Indian rice grass and put it in his mouth.

"Well, you got lots of cedars. Always a demand for fence posts. Some good trees in here for logs for buildings. There's a small cabin just down here," he pointed down the narrow ridge to the south. "Rumor it was built by the Shanes about twenty or so years ago when they came here with sheep. Probably half fallen down now. Nice level spot—not much of that up here."

"Haven't seen a cedar yet that grows big enough to make a log out of," Thad answered. He swatted a fly that kept landing on his arm.

"You walk down the middle draw and you got some big straight ones, almost like pine. Not like these gnarly old bastards up here on the ridge. There's a little water seeping out the hillside, and the bottoms of all three draws are wet. I think seeping from the irrigation up north. Get more irrigation on the mesa and I bet you get more water coming out here. Let's walk around some."

Thad and Tater spent the next two hours wandering the eighty acres. Thad was thinking of how his step-daughter could possibly make a living here. Not much feed for livestock, no water to speak of, and where the water was, it was steep and brushy, too far downhill to even bring up. No access to most of the property for a truck or wagon, tough even for a mule. It did have a nice view, but how could a person make a living sitting there staring off into the distant mountains?

There was no evidence of past forest fires. There were a lot of the gnarly old junipers, a few pinyon, and thick stands of sagebrush on the four almost-level ridgetops. And lots of rocks: huge boulders, smaller rocks, and the ground littered with pebbles. Everything seemed to be covered with colorful lichens and green spongy moss. The land sloped steeply once you dropped off the ridgetops. There were trickles of water in the streambeds, although it didn't appear there was steady flow; it was all spring-fed since there was no water coming down the upper ends of the draws. This area did seem to be natural—untouched by any efforts to tame it. The old cabin and the so-called road were the only signs of human activity—plus the small arrowhead Thad picked up on the northeast sagebrush flat. Lots of deer sign, which meant an easy shot if you wanted to put in a supply of meat.

Tater had a few head of cattle, sheep and pigs on his 120 acres three miles northwest. But he was killing himself trying to make a living off them. And he had flat land, cleared of rocks, and shares of the scarce irrigation water.

"Tater, why ain't nobody filed on this?"

"Well good Jesus, Thad, why do you think? How you gonna make a living off this? Only thing this land is good for is to bury the poor soul that tries to earn his bread up here. And I sure don't want to be the person to try and dig the grave." Tater let out a bellow and slapped Thad on the back as they returned to the pickup.

Later that afternoon, Thad drove up to his house. Della was bringing in the laundry from the clotheslines strung between two big old cottonwood trees. They sat on the porch bench and he described the land and Tater's parting comments. Della responded, "that might be just right for Opal. She needs to get out on her own and have time to think and figure out what she wants to do." Thad said that was no way for a young woman to live, but anything to get her out of the house was alright with him.

When Opal came home from babysitting one of Ruth's boys, Thad told her about the place up on Bean Ridge. She said she wanted to see it. Thad had to go to the bull sale in Dawson the next day, but he said he would take her up there Saturday.

Opal kept to herself most of Friday, passing on the invite to go to the sale. Thad was thankful, since having her with him for something like that made him nervous. He noticed the looks and whispers other folks made when they saw Opal. They knew she was his step-daughter, but where was her husband? Wasn't she the one who ran off to California with a man, then came back alone? Thad didn't want to answer any questions about her.

Saturday morning a thunderstorm was building to the south and moving toward Bean Ridge and Thad and Opal. He parked the truck on the shoulder of the county-maintained road and said, "we'll walk down to the property. I don't want to chance getting down to the end of the track and have a downpour turn it all to mud." Opal didn't say anything, although Thad knew she thought he should go ahead and drive down the track.

She was wearing boots; she usually did, even when she went to town. When they were halfway down—about a quarter mile—they saw an unfamiliar battered pickup approaching them from the property. Opal looked at Thad, "I didn't think anyone lived down here."

"Don't knows anyone does. Maybe a neighbor looking for cows." Thad thought he recognized the truck. When it got closer, he smiled. "It's old Willy Long."

"Who is he?" Opal asked, looking at Thad, then at the driver of the approaching truck.

"Crazy old coot, but guess he isn't that old. Rumor was he got gassed in the War and is a little off. Sticky-fingered and good-for-nothing. Don't know what he'd be doing up here other than stealing somethin'."

The truck came to a stop and a middle-aged man got out. He was wearing faded torn overalls, boots with holes in both toes, and a floppy felt hat. He took the hat off and wiped his face with a red bandanna he pulled out of his back pocket.

"Hi, folks. Say, aren't you Thad Akins?"

"Yes. This is my step-daughter, Opal. Opal, this is Willy Long, isn't it?" He held out his hand to shake Willy's.

"Glad to meet you, Opal. Yep, I'm Willy." He reached out to shake Thad's hand, then Opal's. "What brings you down to my place?"

"Your place? You own this?" Thad said, wondering what Willy would say since he knew Willy didn't own it.

"Well, I'm staying here for now." He laughed and turned around to look back at the building storm. "Old cabin down there. Call it home for now, but it ain't mine. Don't know who built it, but I've done a little fixin' up on 'er. I guess the government owns the land, but what do they want it for?" He laughed and wiped his forehead again. "Not good for nothin'. Just for watching the storms roll in, which looks like we got one coming now." He laughed, which brought on a fit of coughing that brought out the bandanna.

"So you live here. How long you been up here?" Thad wondered what this information would do to the chances of getting the land for Opal.

"Oh, I've only been staying here part of the time. Old lady kicked me out of my own house, so I found this place. Moved my stuff up here a few months ago. Haven't wintered yet, so don't know if I'll stay when the snow comes."

"Were you going to apply for homestead? I heard this property is open for the taking." Thad was hesitant to say this, but he needed to know the answer.

"Oh hell no. I don't need to own this. Ain't worth what it would cost to settle it. Only good for a few goats and skunks." He wheezed as he laughed. "You interested?"

"Don't know. Wanted to come down and take a look around. You mind if we do?"

"I don't own it so I don't have no say. Nothin' worth stealing in the cabin, so go ahead and look in there, too."

"Well, I think we will. Looks like we better hurry or we might get caught in the storm. Lightning already over by Black Canyon. I don't think we're in your way up by the road. Can you get by all right?"

Willy looked past Opal. "No problem. This old jalopy is like an old goat, can go anywhere. You folks have a nice day. If you wanna kick me off, give me a couple days notice." He laughed again and tipped his old hat to Opal as he got back in his truck. It sputtered a few seconds before it started. Thad and Opal stood off to the edge of the track as Willy drove by. He winked at Opal after he drove past Thad. Opal smiled at him, almost laughing out loud.

They stood watching Willy drive out to the road, then turn right and head down off the mesa. "Crazy old coot, but seems harmless enough," Thad said as they continued walking down the track.

"You keep calling him old. He doesn't seem that old to me. Seemed friendly enough. Kinda dirty, though." Opal didn't admit to Thad that she found Willy interesting. She liked his carefree attitude. She wondered about his health; he seemed overweight and his wheezing was obvious. But if it were true about his being gassed in the War, that made sense. On the other hand, why would his wife kick him out? She wanted to learn more about this man.

They wandered around the property for an hour or so, to the ends of the ridges and even down to the three small creeks. There was a little water, with cattails and sumac lining the creeks. There was an abundance of young juniper, and downed junipers and dead branches made walking difficult. When they walked out the main ridge, they marveled at the silver poplar grove north of the cabin. Opal took a lot of interest in the cabin. It was not so old or in that bad of shape. The roof leaked and there was chinking missing from some of the walls, but the windows were new and the door shut. She opened the door to peek in, but wouldn't walk in. Thad admonished her not to pry in someone else's house, even if they were trespassing and didn't own the place.

Over the past half hour, the wind had picked up and a few sprinkles of rain fell. The main storm seemed stuck down in the valley but was now edging closer to them. As they walked back up the track to Thad's truck, lightning struck a mile to the west. Opal walked with a new bounce in her step. She sensed the possibilities of this place. Thad noticed this, especially when she started whistling. He had never heard her whistle before. She looked back over her shoulder several times.

A lightning bolt hit within a half-mile as Thad and Opal slammed the doors and settled on the seat. "Whew," Thad let out a breath. "That was kind of close. Made it just in time." He started the truck and pulled into the road. "Well, Opal, you seem cheerful. You like the place?"

"No." She paused. Thad looked at her in surprise and started to say something but Opal continued. "I love the place. I can fix up the cabin, and I can have chickens, a couple pigs, some goats..." She trailed off, deep in thought.

"What about that Willy? You would have to kick him out. I don't like the looks of him. Never did. He always seems to avoid decent people."

"I think he is an interesting character," Opal said, half-smiling. "Hmmm...maybe 'resourceful'," she said as she stumbled to find the right word.

"Oh my God, Opal, how can you think that? Or even useful in any way. He is filthy and a bum and has a reputation as a thief." Thad shifted in his seat as he continued down the dirt road off the mesa. He scrunched his eyes and looked at her. She laughed. It had been a long time since Thad heard her laugh. "Oh, Thad, I don't mean he's good to look at—he is ugly. And I don't mean he's upright or a good person. But he seems so carefree, even happy. I bet nothing worries him. Living up here by himself, with all this to look at." She waved at the distant mountains, now partially obscured by sheets of rain.

Opal wanted to be off by herself. Living a comfortable life was not a priority. She wanted to be in charge, not dependent on anyone . This place felt good for those few things that were important to her. She would figure out details later, knowing she could handle something like this. After all, she'd managed for a while in Oakland, proved that to herself and to Alberto. "Oh my God," she cringed when that thought crossed her mind. Alberto. "What would he think of this?"

Thad glanced again at Opal. She was surprising him. Maybe this was what she needed. She was opening up to him like she hadn't before. He still didn't like the idea of Willy being there.

"You really like it up here, don't you? It's not that much different from our place."

He immediately regretted saying that. He wanted her to get out on her own, so he shouldn't do anything to keep her from settling up here. He still preferred she do it the traditional way, by marrying some rancher and settling down. But he knew that would not happen. She'd had her experience with marriage and things went very wrong; Opal was too independent to do that again. Things worked out more often than they didn't. Especially in this country where it took a partnership and family to make ends meet. A widower like him and an abandoned wife and mother like Della seemed to naturally find each other. They needed each other and love and attraction were not always that important—marriage in this time and place was more a partnership to survive. Based on everything Della had told him, Thad thought that Opal should never have gone to the big city. But that was Opal—you couldn't tell her anything. Thad's musings lead him to wonder if it was something more than independence: had something affected her mind?

Opal interrupted Thad's train of thought. "I want to come back here and sit and think on this. I like it up here and think I could make a go of this place. It's secluded, hardly any neighbors, has some water, some grass. I can grow a garden, too. I don't mind hard work." What she didn't say was that just maybe, she might get some help out of Willy. He could help her build a bigger cabin, and she might let him stay, provided he helped around the place. She laughed to herself thinking she might get a laborer as part of the deal.

~

In the early years of what became known as Bean Ridge, no settlers lived on the mesa. Pioneer ranchers coming into the area swarmed the valley and the lower mesas as soon as the government kicked out the Utes—the rightful inhabitants of the area for thousands of years. Unlike the Utes, who found all land useful and sacred, few of the white newcomers ventured up onto this dry expanse of juniper and sagebrush. There was no permanent water and since this was a genuine mesa, not the sloping tablelands below—incorrectly labeled mesas—it was not practical to grow anything other than natural grass, which before the overgrazing by cattle, was abundant.

During a few wet years at the turn of the century, some homesteaders planted apple trees, which grew well for a few years; some of the draws ran a little water part of the year, so ditches were dug and hopes were high. Ranchers began filing to obtain title through the Homestead Act; but without more water, the land was still marginal, and work began to ditch water miles from the nearby mountains.

By the 1920s, things had changed little from the days decades ago when the valley was overrun with white settlers after the removal of the Utes. Opal had grown up with lots of new farmers and ranchers moving to the valley and mesas from Missouri and Illinois and other points east. She never gave a thought as to how they got the land. "It was unfair to the Utes, but they are gone, so someone has to live here—might as well be me," she smiled to herself.

The next day, Opal hitched a ride and came back to sit and ponder and walk all around and up and down the land again—dreaming of all kinds of possibilities. But more importantly, she would be by herself, not dependent on anyone. She would figure out how to make a living up here. She told the ravens and jays and chickadees, "I made it on my own in California and can do it again here. No Alberto to help me now, but I learned confidence with his guidance. I can get it back!"

Thad loaned his pickup to Opal several days later to drive to Montrose to visit officials at the U.S. government General Land Office. He was a little hesitant to let her borrow the truck, but Della said it would be good for her. Opal hadn't driven a vehicle for several years and had little experience before that. In California, She had been nervous behind the wheel, especially Alberto's luxury Kissel Speedster; he'd taught her to drive but his expensive car made her uncomfortable. She preferred to rest her shoulder against Alberto as he drove in the Berkeley Hills. On this day, the roads were not good and she drove very slowly.

The Montrose General Land Office was responsible for administering the homestead process in western Colorado. The land Opal wanted to file on was one of the last parcels available for homesteading. And for good reasons: mostly juniper- and sage-covered, it was too steep, uneven, dry, and rocky for any commercial use. And rumor had it that the homestead program was about to end. No one knew who built the log cabin that Opal took possession of along with the property. Nor did anyone know when it was built, and as Opal and Thad had seen, it was in rough shape.

Opal picked up the paperwork and discussed the protocol with Mr. Dickinson, the homestead administrator.

"Are you sure you understand the process?" he asked her. "It can be rather complicated. You have to live on the property for five years. You have to show you can make a living there." He had to repeat the question several times before she answered, she was so nervous, and she had to repeat her answers before she convinced him that she did understand. "Yes, I do. I want my own land. I will raise pigs and chickens. There's already a cabin there."

Mr. Dickinson was surprised there was a building there, although this often happened since squatting and trespass were common on the government parcels close to towns and settlements.

Opal was energized, for the first time in over a year. She felt good— eager to move onto the land. She could borrow money from Della and buy a couple weaner pigs, and some chicks from the Beaver Creek feed store. But, before she could think about the details required to prove up the land, Opal had to decide what to do about Willy. She hadn't talked to him for several weeks. Previously he'd said he was more than happy to leave the cabin—that there were other areas he could go. There was empty land up by Uncle Tater, as well as a section a few miles west, near Enos Wilson's place. On the other hand, she needed help with making her new place work.

After spending that evening and the next filling out the forms, Opal rode with Thad to the Beaver Creek post office and mailed the paperwork, then he took her up to the homestead. Willy was sitting on the front door step of the cabin, and said he'd bring Opal back to Wolf Park before supper.

~

As Opal sat down on the other end of the step, she told Willy she'd filed the homestead papers, and that if he would help her build some fencing and a small chicken coop, he could stay for a while. "I like you,

Willy, although I think you are a strange character. I don't believe what some folks say about you."

Willy shifted uneasily, wondering what some folks were saying. He could guess, and he really didn't care. "Miss Opal, I'm just like you. I got gassed and kicked around. You got beat down and kicked around." He laughed, then turned his head and spit on the ground beside him.

"Thad says he will help me build a proper house. But I know he won't if you stay. I'd like you to stick around and help me some. So I will just add onto the cabin here. Can you help me bring in some logs?"

"Well, Miss Opal," Willy started to say.

"Let's stop with the Miss Opal. My name is Opal and you call me Opal. Do you understand that?" She leaned back after moving right into Willy's face to reprimand him. She squinted her eyes at the smell of his breath. It reminded her of a pack rat nest she found under a big rock down the ridge.

"Yes ma'am," Willy said as he pulled out his bandanna. He stuffed it back in his pocket after wiping his chin, then he pulled out a tin of chewing tobacco and put a wad in his mouth.

"I know a spot up Leroux Creek where we can get a couple loads of quakies. Up on the Forest. Rangers never get up there so we can get some good ones without paying."

"No, Willy, if we have to pay, we pay. I want to do things right and proper."

"You're in charge, I guess," Willy said lamely.

"Yes, I am in charge, and don't you ever forget that. I set the rules. I am allowing you to stay here. But you understand one thing. Don't expect sex. Never. You understand that?" She stood up as she said that. She suddenly pulled up her shirt, exposing her scar, including her breasts. Willy almost jumped up in shock. "This came from having sex with an evil beast of a man. He hurt me and left me with this." She let her shirt down and turned her back to him.

Willy, still surprised, stuttered. "My God, Miss, I mean Opal. What happened?"

"You will never know. All you know is I ain't never getting close to a man again. Those are the rules. Understand?"

"Well, you don't need to worry about me. I'd show you my reasons for not being interested either, but it's too much trouble to take down my pants. War did more than gas me." He turned and spit, then wiped his mouth with his sleeve.

Willy vaguely remembered Opal from years before when she was growing up in this area. He hadn't known her but had heard about her independent nature. He watched her closely as she lectured him. She was still an attractive young woman but was letting herself go. He felt relieved that she was accepting him on his own terms and abilities, and that there was no attraction to her physically.

He had two half-grown sons and an ex-wife living somewhere nearby, but Willy never talked about them and they never came to see him. Opal heard from someone that he was never actually married to the woman and she kicked him out. Opal didn't care to talk to him about it, so any details remained forever unknown to her. She did not tell Willy of her life in California either, so both could start their lives over.

Opal held out her hand. "Let's shake on a business proposition." They shook hands. Opal cringed as she wiped her hand after grasping Willy's tobacco-stained hand. Willy smiled, then wheezed.

Three

Opal had learned to navigate the bus and train systems back in the Bay Area of California, but didn't have those transportation luxuries in Beaver County. Half the time, the roads on—and up to—Bean Ridge were too muddy or snow-covered to reach Beaver Creek. Another casualty from her California experience was her aversion to cities and even towns. She could take the train from Beaver Creek into Dawson or Grand Junction, but they were big cities as far as she was concerned. "No need to go there," she would mutter when someone might mention them. Even though she'd never seen a town of more than a few hundred people when she landed in Oakland, she had adjusted. Now, she avoided people like deer avoid cougar.

Willy's old truck ran, but it seemed he was always tinkering with it. Opal counted on him driving to town or to get supplies. As time went on, she left the property less and less. Her world now consisted of her eighty acres of trees, sagebrush, cattails, the creeks, the birds, a couple of pigs and goats, a hound dog, two scruffy cats, and the view of the nearby and the far-off mountains. Her world shrunk steadily every year, although her memories hung on by a slender thread.

At first, Opal would not let Willy sleep in the small cabin. It was autumn, so he slept in a makeshift tent he erected. The tarp showed up one day and Opal didn't ask questions. She accepted his presence just as she accepted the goats and chickens; he could be useful in doing some things around the place; he was occasionally annoying; and he occasionally found excuses for getting out of really hard work. Willy became part of the landscape. Opal knew she would never find another Alberto and she never even thought of trying to.

~

A stack of old boards and a few new slabs from the mill down by the river appeared one day. The slabs were good as rough-cut boards, with a little bark on one side. Willy and Opal easily found four straight, small-diameter cedars within walking distance of the cabin, sawed them down and trimmed off the few branches. Willy was becoming good at digging holes, and set the cedars as corner posts for a shed. A week later, while Willy was off who-knows-where, Opal, on her own, had a small shed nailed together on the posts, plus a roof.

When Willy returned he exclaimed, "Lord, Opal, you get this done all by yourself?" and set a box of nails on the ground. "Brought you some more nails. Good as new, though a little rusty."

"Where'd you get these? They all bent up?"

"Hell no woman. They're brand new. From the new Baker house down by the river. Found this box off in the weeds. They must've forgot it. House is all built and this here box just sitting there waiting to be used by somebody. Might as well be you. Us." Willy smiled as he wiped his face with his bandana.

"How do you find these things, Willy? You spend all your time lookin', then stealin?"

"Damnation, woman, I don't steal nothin'. These were forgot about. Goin' to waste. Why not use them? No one will ever know. You don't want 'em, I'll give 'em to someone else. Don't tell me we can't use 'em. You can't afford to buy a box like that." Willy frowned at Opal as he stuffed a new wad of tobacco in his mouth.

Opal still didn't approve of Willy's foraging. But, the strangest things showed up. Some were legitimate, like the box of nails. Many were just plain stolen. Willy would grin and tell people he had borrowed whatever they came looking for. He seemed to think it was a game. If he got caught, that was fine. If not, then his 'appropriating' paid off. Most of his prizes were junk, but occasionally a shovel, a roll of fencing wire, a car part, a bale of hay would show up. Even these were usually old, used, or not in very good shape. But still—Opal pondered—it wasn't proper.

It didn't bother Opal that everything was cobbled together. The cabin, fences, animal pens, her garden, the track that served as a road. She couldn't afford to buy much of anything new. And with Willy providing most of what they needed, they made do. If he was getting the reputation of a comical bumbling 'borrower'—which included her by association—then so be it. She wasn't trying to impress anyone and was way beyond caring what other folks thought.

Over time she was mentally leaving California behind, including the only reason she had ever had to be proud of herself—Alberto and his love and respect for her. She still treasured the three record albums that reminded her of Alberto—keeping some positive memories alive, and those memories may be what kept Opal functioning.

For a while, she thought about what was happening to her on the homestead. She was better than this and had proved it in California, with Alberto. But that was gone. Gone forever. How could she think living with Willy was an acceptable alternative? Because their mutual acceptance of each other was helping her forget her past life.

With as much work as Willy put in on expanding and improving the cabin and other projects, Opal began to feel guilty making him sleep under the tarp. As the fall of that first year cooled the nights to freezing, she told Willy he could sleep inside, as long as he got another bed and at least hung a blanket to divide the small bedroom. She knew he snored; she could hear him from outside. What she didn't know was she could match his decibel output. The deer and foxes would look at the cabin with perked ears as they wandered by in the dark—and the noisy reputation of the cabin spread throughout the animal community.

Before Opal cleaned the cabin and made plans to increase its size, she sought advice from Thad and Della, her sister Ruth and brother Preston, but mostly she listened to Willy. Della shook her head whenever Opal even mentioned Willy's name. On one of her rare visits to her ma at Wolf Park, while working together in the vegetable garden, she commented that Willy was helping her in many ways on the homestead. Della scoffed and said, "Opal, dear, that man is worthless. Your husband was cruel to you and he was evil, but Willy is lazy. He is harmless, but he is a bum."

"Ma, you have no right to lecture me. Look who you settled on. Pa was no saint."

"Opal, you are still my daughter. You have no right..." She stopped picking the few remaining cucumbers, sat back on her heels, and looked at Opal from under the brim of her gardening hat. She was as close to slapping Opal as she had ever come. "I made a mistake, just like you. But I learned from it. I set things right. Thad is as good as they come. You might treat him with a little more respect."

"If he had respect for you, he would get out of your bed. All he wants is to keep you pregnant. My God, you are so worn out that for Dinah you were out of milk and couldn't nurse anymore and had to have Ruth breastfeed her." She knew she had stepped over the line when Della stood up and strode to Opal, overcame her hesitation and slapped her on the face, then turned and covered her own face with her hands.

"Opal, I am sorry, but you have no right. I am responsible for your life, no matter how old you are. You are not responsible for my life. At least not yet. Maybe someday…"

~

Both Thad and Della had to acknowledge the change in Opal: she was accepting responsibility for her new home. She had never seemed to care about much of anything before. Now she did. Della and Thad visited the place one day while Opal was trying to put up a fence. They were bringing Opal several chickens. A coyote had gotten into their chicken coop and nearly wiped out their flock. Thad was so disgusted, he wanted to get rid of the birds for awhile; they weren't laying much anyway and he wanted to rebuild the coop. He told Della they could take the few remaining birds up to Opal, then start over in the spring.

When Thad and Della arrived, Opal was struggling to stretch and flatten a mess of old chicken wire. Willy was nowhere in sight.

"Opal, where is Willy ?" Thad asked quietly.

"Dunno," Opal muttered through the fence staples in her mouth.

"Wouldn't it be easier for him to help you? This really is a two-person job." Della picked up one end of the wire and held it tight.

"Willy isn't here. I don't need no one to help." Opal pounded a staple into a tree trunk, then cursed as it bounced out after she hit her thumb. She put the dirty thumb in her mouth, then looked at it as a purple bruise blossomed.

Thad turned away so they couldn't see him laugh. Poor Opal, he thought. She is learning, although the hard way. He thought about helping, but instead, he turned around and said, "Well Della, we need to get going. Opal, we brought you these birds. Still laying some, but not much. When they quit, you can eat them. They need to be protected at night. I'm sure you got as many foxes and coyotes as we got. Saw a Great Horned owl the last time I was here, plus you got more eagles than we do. Lots of things other than yourself want to eat these ladies. Should be enough grasshoppers and bugs for them, but they would do better with a little feed. Store in Beaver Creek has some on sale this week."

"Well, my lord Thad, we can't leave now. Opal needs help," Della protested. "And she can't afford to buy no feed. Didn't you bring her any?"

Thad picked a long stem of wheatgrass and put it in his mouth. "Della, Opal doesn't want help. She can do all this by herself. That lazy Willy should be up here. More'n likely he is out 'borrowing' something from somebody right now. Right, Opal?"

Opal shot him a stare that could have set his grass stem on fire. She finally found the staple she was searching for on the ground and pounded it in the tree. The chicken wire was now stretched but needed tightening with a few more posts.

Della let go and walked back to Thad. She punched him in the ribs as she walked past him to get in the truck. Thad smiled. "Opal, that fence will have to be twice as high to keep out the critters. They can hop over a pretty tall fence." Thad set the crate of birds on the ground and threw out two sacks of feed grain. "These gals have been pretty good to us. Talk nice to them and they might be good to you for awhile." He grinned and got in the truck, backed around and drove up the track. Della looked out and waved to Opal, but Opal was busy pounding staples into a two by four.

~

More animals kept appearing as their on-the-hoof food store. Besides the chickens her step-father had dropped off, Opal's menagerie expanded to include more pigs and goats, two milk cows, a mule, two ewes, a collie dog, and three hen turkeys.

Although the eighty acres extended across four ridgetops and three watered draws, there was not much natural feed for all the domestic animals they had. And the smaller ones provided more feed for predators than for Opal and Willy. Every time a chicken disappeared, Opal went to the tool shed grumbling. She would grab a scrap of chicken wire and patch up holes in the fence. After the first year, Opal's fences were cobbled together by so many versions and variations of chicken wire, baling wire, barbed wire, smooth wire, rope, hog wire, boards, and rusted truck and auto parts, that they blended into the landscape. A neighbor who hadn't been on the property for several years climbed over the fence on the east side looking for two of his goats that had disappeared. He dropped his jaw when he saw the mazes running up and down the hillsides, across the creek, and winding around the cabin. He quietly left, knowing he would most likely not see his goats again.

The fencing complemented the patchwork of old car parts, barrels, scrap metal, stacks of boards, and other assorted junk that accumulated over time. Of course there was no county dump, so for Opal all cans, bottles, and non-burnable junk went down the hillside east of the cabin. At first, Opal didn't like the idea of using the hillside as a dump, but after getting used to seeing the garbage, after awhile she failed to notice it anymore.

~

In three years, Opal and Willy had transformed what was a pristine piece of the mesa into a junkyard—which paralleled what Opal had transformed herself into. One morning, she looked in a rearview mirror on a junk car Willy had pulled onto the property. She gasped when she saw what she now looked like. A mess: long hair tangled, scratches across her dirty face, clothes torn and patched. She hadn't worn makeup since she last saw Alberto. She rarely brushed her teeth and they were getting stained and yellow. What used to be a small spot on her nose was starting to grow as a wart. Opal was barely 30 years old but she looked 50.

She stepped back from the mirror—shocked. Tears welled in her eyes. She brushed her hair back and rubbed her nose. "Oh my God," she said to herself. "What happened?" This wasn't what she wanted, but she had no idea what she did want. Yes, she did. She wanted to be back in San Francisco with Alberto. She gulped, blinked back tears, then wept.

"No, no, no, no," she thought. She wiped her eyes and looked around. No one should be anywhere near, but she had to check anyway. "I'll never cry again," she said to herself. "Never." She was independent, fully in charge of her life. She might live by herself (Willy didn't count; she kept justifying his presence), but she would never have to depend on anyone else. It didn't occur to her that whenever they needed to spend money on something, it was the money sent to Willy by the U.S. Government as pension and disability pay for his service in the War. He never talked about having been horribly wounded in France, but he expected the check, he deserved it, and that was that.

Their only other income was the monthly cream check from the local dairy and a few dollars from selling fence posts they cut from the junipers on their place. Although they actually got some milk from the cows in late summer and early fall, a good portion was from the goats—even though they certified to the dairy that the milk came from dairy cows. For several years, Opal hitched rides down to the fruit packing sheds and worked in the orchards, first picking, then packing apples. She saved every penny she earned, stuffing her income into a half-gallon canning jar under her bed. However, when they had to spend money on anything, Opal would complain to Willy that she didn't have any money. Willy always came up with some cash; none of it from Opal's jar.

Not included in Opal's finances was the remaining shipping company and insurance money from Paul's death benefits. Early on, she had spent some, but most (with Della's help) she had converted to gold coins, stashed in a quart-size canning jar and buried outside the cabin. Distrusting banks, she drew a map, marked the spot with two white stones, and figured this was Opal's Bank. She knew it would come in handy someday. What she didn't plan on was: 1) losing the map; 2) not realizing Willy moved the rocks; and 3) eventually forgetting about the money. As the years went by, remembrance of the jar and its contents left Opal's consciousness.

Della came up occasionally to visit, and grew disturbed over Opal's gradual decline. She gave bolts of material to Opal to make dresses, but Opal refused to put on a dress. She wore pants and shirts that Willy brought her. Her floppy felt hat was a Willy-reject; he was now sporting a wide-brimmed straw Stetson. Della knew all too well that a working ranch wife was rough on clothes and needed nothing different from her man. "But my God," she thought, "a woman has to have something nice to remind herself she is a woman—if only for church on Sunday mornings. But since Opal hasn't seen the inside of a church in years, well, when then?" The new Grange down the road had dances at least once a month, but Opal refused to enter the building. Opal would occasionally dance, in a manner of speaking, to her Puccini records that she played on the hand-crank player. The music wasn't exactly dancing music, but she had swirled around the hotel room in Alberto's arms after that one evening at the opera in San Francisco.

~

On a spring day in '35, Opal received a notice in the mailbox of a registered letter. She had Willy drive her into Beaver Creek where a large manila envelope with a fancy design around the edge waited for her. She signed her name and took the envelope from the Postmaster. He jokingly asked her what award she was receiving from the President. Only then did she notice the mail was postmarked Washington D.C., Department of the Interior. She thanked him and walked out of the Post Office, the official staring at this disheveled woman as she climbed into Willy's pickup. She had no idea what the contents might be as she ripped open the envelope. There was a letter with lots of bureaucratic writing, and, accompanying it was a deed to her property. Opal now owned her 80 acres. The signature on the deed was Franklin D. Roosevelt, President of the United States. She had proved up on her homestead. She let out a whoop that echoed down Main Street.

Willy's reaction was to step on the gas to get out of town as soon as possible. "My God, woman, you got ants crawling up your pants?"

"You treat me with respect old man. I am a landowner. Drive me out to Thad and Della's place. I got to show this to Ma."

Della hugged her tightly, but her first comment was, "Opal dear, now you will have to pay taxes. You got the money for that?" Della still had mixed feelings about Opal and Willy, but at least Opal no longer asked her and Thad for money.

~

Over the years, the mesa's ditch company expanded its water supply with small reservoirs up on the mountain, but Opal still couldn't afford to buy a share in the irrigation water company. She and Willy did all right by diverting the tailwater from the neighbors' fields as it left them, and they managed to irrigate the large garden area north of the cabin.

The land was uniquely suited to benefit from this free water: it was downhill from those fields and topographically the water could not go back into the ditch company system. Her property was the only place for it to go—and she didn't have to pay for it. Willy laughed whenever he read in the paper about ditch rates going up per share. "Let those farmers pay for developing the ditches and reservoirs. We don't pay a thing and we get a little bit of free water," he said sarcastically. It wasn't enough to grow much more than cabbage and potatoes, but at least it was free; in Willy's mind, that was the only thing that mattered.

Opal spent hours spading and weeding the garden, and she did fairly well in canning a variety of vegetables: her own cabbage and potatoes and apricots, other fruit (seconds of course) from the packing shed, and the excess from Ma's garden. She canned so much that she asked Willy to dig a root cellar next to the cabin. She had never seen him work so hard. The digging was moving as much rock as soil. Of course, Willy complained the whole time, but that first year she was able to fill four shelves with dozens of quarts of canned beans, tomatoes, potatoes, sauerkraut, carrots, and fruit preserves.

Stooping to enter the dirt cellar, Opal paused to let her eyes adjust to the darkness. On a hot September afternoon, the cool, earthen cave felt refreshing. As she eyed the food jars, she smiled. No matter what had happened to the bright young lady of San Francisco, she thought, she had mastered something. She could live by herself on her own land. Maybe she could survive in the big city, wearing fancy gowns and sitting in the opera, but she was queen up here. Let Paul see her now. Why could she not throw out the memories of that man? She didn't want him to mar her thoughts. She had to toss him out completely.

The Depression raged in the outside world, but Opal didn't notice much in her little world on the mesa. This whole area was dirt poor—people called Bean Ridge a Little Appalachia. Living in poverty was a way of life, so Opal fit right in.

Four

Having shut the dogs in the cabin so they wouldn't follow, Opal walked south along the ridge sloping gently down from her cabin. Enjoying the warmth of spring sunshine, she picked her way among the sagebrush, small junipers and lichen-covered boulders. She thought back to a similar day three years previously on a walk to this place that she considered her secret place. She had spent her first two years on her very own property and needed a break from the cabin and her chores, which increased daily. Memories of that day stayed with her, and aspects of her life slowly changed in importance. She liked exploring the property and discovered something new each day.

On that walk three years ago, she realized she had never actually noticed the rocks before, or at least not in detail. The low morning sunlight had highlighted the lichen, pasted like children's paintings in vibrant colors on the grayish-black boulders: white and black, with oranges, yellows, and greens and grays clumping and swirling in tight blankets and peeling flakes. They were alive!—growing on rocks and tree limbs and even sagebrush branches. "What is the true color of the rock?" she had asked herself.

Now, five years since returning from California, Opal found a large boulder with a curved depression on top just right to fit her still-thin fanny. She nestled on it with her feet dangling, not quite touching the bare reddish-brown soil below. She noticed her left boot was untied. Did she forget to tie it or did it come undone? She didn't know. "Getting sloppy," she thought. It didn't bother her that she didn't care it was untied. This reminded her of days in her childhood, so distant in memory if not time, when she would sit on a rock near home and day-dream about far-off places. She mused aloud, "Why can't things happen as they do in day-dreams?"

She gazed across the valley below. Overhead, stringers of clouds drifted slowly east. The air smelled fresh. That made her think of the salt and fish smell of the Bay. She still missed the cry of the seagulls. They had gotten on her nerves at the time, but they meant the ocean and the ocean made her think of Alberto. She thought of that one time on his sailboat and smiled with the memory of his tanned body along-side her pale one. The spacious view from Alberto's house in the Berkeley Hills was similar to this—but instead of bay, city, and ocean, she now saw the distant jagged peaks of the San Juan Mountains, gray-blue in the remnants of last night's storm, with the vastness of space beyond, and the valley floor filled with orchards, small farms, cattle, hedge rows, and alfalfa fields. No matter how hard she tried, she could not let go of the good times she shared in that earlier setting and time in the Bay Area. "Never again," she sighed. "Gotta get over it," she told herself once again. She feared she never would.

The ocean should have made her think of that scum Paul, but it didn't. He had used the ocean to escape, to spread his ugliness, and to get away from her; it eventually swallowed him up and good riddance. She thought of the sea as a cleansing thing. Alberto had erased the ugliness of Paul. And now she had to erase the good thoughts of Alberto—the one good thing to happen in her life and he too was gone. It was not fair, she thought—then aloud, "It's not fair!"

Opal looked up as an eagle's shadow crossed directly over, the bird flying low, and chirping loudly. Opal watched it bank north and fly over the cabin. She heard a raven scold it following in pursuit. She laughed as three more ravens joined the chase. The eagle kept going, twisting and turning to fend off the black harassers. "I'm the eagle and the ravens are my bad memories. I'll ignore them and keep circling...climb higher and keep to myself," she thought.

A chipmunk scampered across a nearby rock, then climbed on a low branch of a large spreading juniper. It chattered at her, flicking its tail to accompany its barks. "What are you telling me, flip-tail? I guess you are scolding me just like everyone else has."

The chipmunk flicked its tail a few more times, ran down the tree and disappeared. She could hear it scolding further down the hill. It was soon joined in chorus by a chickadee. "Scold me all you want, don't matter no more to me. You better be nice to me. I'm the only friend you have and you may be the only ones I have."

She thought about friends. There were none here except Willy and Ma. Maybe Ruth, and Thad. Far away were Mabel and Francine in Oakland, and Betty in Long Beach. But she had to forget about California; for her it didn't exist anymore. As hard as she tried, she could not quite forget that past life, and she could never love anyone again. She would just live up here—with the eagles and ravens and chipmunks. Ignore the bad things, like the eagle did the ravens. She could tolerate Willy. She would never love him and he probably didn't know what love was. Because of his war injuries, he wasn't interested in sex, certainly not love.

Watching the eagle join another high in the blueness overhead, Opal thought about the last four years—living up here on Bean Ridge, the proud owner of land, trees, eagles, and chipmunks. She had started over. Why couldn't she forget about her past? No matter what she saw or thought of, those years and the people, both good and bad, kept haunting her. "I have to let go. Totally forget. Why can't I?"

~

Opal had left Colorado nine years earlier, a day-dreaming country girl, bored, but constrained by the wide-open spaces of Beaver County. She had never fit in with her brother and sister, was always at odds with her mother, and hated her father Whitney.

According to him, Opal was impetuous and sassy. Aloof to what was going on, her mind was always wandering. Though pretty, tall and thin, with braided long brown hair, in high school the town boys made fun of her. But that lasted only until she jumped a lanky red-haired boy, sat on him, pounded his face with her fists, broke a couple of his teeth and dislocated his shoulder, before a teacher pulled her off. Whitney came into town and successfully pleaded with the principal to let her stay in school rather than be expelled; but as soon as she got home, he lashed her back with a leather belt, leaving scars that remained for the rest of her life.

Not long after, on a sunny October morning, Opal fell to day-dreaming while helping her father move cows down a fenced lane. She got ahead of the cattle and was walking slowly. Whitney, on horseback, kept yelling at her to get out of the way, that she was spooking the cows and they would not pass her. Finally, he rode up to her, struck her with his cattle whip, and ran her into the fence, cutting her arms on the barbed wire. Opal vowed then that she would leave Beaver County as soon as she could.

But, Whitney left before her. He never fit in either, especially after he burdened Della with three children. Della finally booted him out, although he claimed he got fed up with her insults and left on his own. Leaving a wife and children without any means of support, he disappeared among the growing masses of migrants to southern California, never to be heard of again.

However, the situation didn't improve: Opal didn't fit in. She had to help her mother take care of her brother and do chores, so had little time to socialize with anyone her own age. But it didn't matter since she usually had nothing to say to them and they thought her strange and stand-offish. Opal's day-dreams were of going to somewhere else—New York or California, or even Paris. She had no idea what these places were like and she had never met anyone who had been there, but they still held a fascination that Beaver County did not.

When Opal dressed up for an occasional dance or social, she was an attractive girl. However, she rarely dressed up. Her classmates called her tomboy, but of course not to her face. She was always doing things on a dare, experimenting with the unusual, often to Della's dismay. When Ma called her different, and a problem, Opal did even more daring things.

At age 17, three years after Whitney's departure, during the monthly Saturday night dance at the country church, Opal went to the nearby Thompson barn with Bobby Turner. Bobby pulled off her dress and was on top of her before she had a chance to decide whether to try this new thing. But, being raised on a farm, she was used to seeing animals engage in sex. She knew girls who had done this and they all laughed at her when she admitted she was still a virgin. Bobby obviously had not done this before either. Opal wondered what was so great about it, but the next weekend—out of curiosity—she did it correctly with Freddie Benson along the creek in full daylight.

Over a year later, at the County Fair in Beaver Creek in August, Opal was helping Freddie with his lambs when she met Paul Koenig. He was wearing a sailor cap and a brass-buttoned blue flannel shirt, much too hot for the 90-degree temperatures. He asked her about the lambs and pushed Freddie aside when he tried to answer.

Paul was confident and cocky, which attracted Opal. He talked about the ocean and China and other mysterious places he'd visited as a sailor in the merchant marine. He was from the western edge of the county but had moved to California several years earlier, and was here for a month visit with an aunt and uncle. He sailed mostly out of San Francisco and spent months at sea, usually going to and from the Orient. He walked with Opal over to the food booths and spent several dollars buying her treats, then they went on all the carnival rides together. He kissed her when they stopped on the top of the Ferris wheel, his hands groping under her dress the whole time.

When Opal went home that night, she thought of China and San Francisco, and this good-looking blond-haired sailor. She liked him, especially his confident and worldly manner. She saw him as a way to leave Beaver County. Paul, though older than her, could be her ticket out.

He visited her every day, taking her horseback riding, and going for long rides in his Ford Model A. Della didn't approve of Paul, which attracted Opal even more to him. By this time, Della (having divorced Whitney for desertion) was married to Thad Akins, a widower; he, too, cautioned Opal about the cocky young sailor, but that backfired as well.

Two weeks later, when Paul said he had to return to California and wanted Opal to go with him, she agreed. Della's last words to Opal as Paul threw Opal's suitcase into his car were, "Opal, all I can say as your mother is if you go with him, you will regret it for the rest of your life. He is no good for you."

~

Opal's attention came back to the present and her home on Bean Ridge when she heard a locomotive whistle, far below on Rock Mesa. She could see the puffs of black coal smoke as the train snaked along the river. It was five miles away, but when the wind was just right the sound carried up here, a thousand feet above the valley. The chipmunk was still scolding her from a hidden rock, but the eagles and ravens had disappeared.

She sighed and thought about what Ma had told her the day she drove off with Paul. And Ma had been right—very right. Paul was no good and had ruined her life. She was glad he was dead and in retrospect wished it had happened sooner. As Opal got up from her rock perch, she leaned over and picked up a small red stone and inspected it—sometimes she found shell fossils on them. None in this one, so she tossed it back on the ground and noticed another red rock. Squatting down near it, she picked up a reddish flint arrowhead, and turned it over in her fingers several times, feeling the smooth sides and sharp edges.

"My lucky day," she whispered. She put the arrowhead in the pocket of her faded plaid shirt, made sure the button-flap was secure, and looked on the ground for more. She saw nothing but the small, pocked basalt stones that covered the ridgetop.

Walking back uphill, she stopped suddenly, as something moved on the ground in front of her. It went behind a large boulder. She slowly approached and peered over the top: a large gopher snake was winding into a hole underneath.

"Hey You—Snake! You can't ruin a good thing!" As soon as she said that, she looked skyward and thought about it. "You are good—eatin' vermin, the bane of all farmers! You aren't like that snake, Paul…Slithering into my life…slithering under the nearest rock. Something good happened by finding the arrowhead—by meeting Alberto. Then Paul, that snake ruined it."

Five

"**I should think this all through!**" Opal exclaimed, and made herself comfortable on another boulder. Staring off at the distant mountains, she thought about the *snake* in her life. She had enjoyed the drive across the deserts and mountains of Utah and Nevada and over the Sierra. The roads were bad and the drive was long, but it was somewhere other than Beaver County. She had never experienced such wide-open emptiness as she saw in Utah and Nevada. After a quick marriage in Reno, the long climb up out of the Nevada desert floor and over the summit of Donner Pass was nerve-wracking. Coming down the west side of the Sierra thrilled her—she had never seen such large trees.

Paul was good to her those first days as they traveled, although he often laughed at her when she commented on the view. She started to notice his attitude was demeaning; at first, it didn't bother her. He was a world-traveling adventurer, and she was a naïve country girl who knew nothing. But by Donner Pass, Paul's abusive attitude started to concern her. They stopped often to gas the car or to eat at roadside restaurants. She looked forward to stopping for the night at hotels in the small towns, eating in their restaurants, looking at photographs on the lobby walls. Towns were few and far between, but they reminded her of home. She didn't miss home, but she often thought about it and Ma and the people she grew up with.

Paul took Opal to Oakland, where he had a small apartment near the waterfront. She felt out of place in the city and gaped at people whenever she left the apartment. She liked the smell and sounds of the Bay but told Paul she wanted to see the real ocean, not just the quiet bay. Paul kept saying they would go to the coast, but not yet. Paul made fun of her cooking; she had learned to cook at an elevation of 6000 feet and she struggled to get used to sea level. Her first cakes and cookies, as well as loaves of bread, were embarrassing failures. Paul's harping at her started to take on a new tone as he made fun of her more often.

After three weeks in Oakland, Paul returned to work and sailed off on a four-week trip to Anchorage. He left Opal with only a few dollars and little food in the kitchen. She enjoyed the peace and quiet for several days, but soon the weather turned wet and cold. She tried to light the oil heater but couldn't get it started and asked the landlord for help. He was patient with her as he showed her how to light it, but she overheard him making fun of her as he walked down the sidewalk to his car.

Opal was alone. She couldn't call Ma since Della had no phone, and was too proud to call even if she could. She did write a few letters but made it sound like she was having a great time.

After the third week without Paul, she was miserable. Not from missing him—his absence didn't bother her at all. What caused the problem was that he didn't leave her means to live—no money and she didn't have a job. Not knowing anyone, never mind the culture shock of the Bay Area, she was still struggling to learn city life.

Two days later, a young man in a heavy blue wool coat—like Paul wore—knocked on the door. Opal opened the door but left the screen latched. The man said his name was Art and he sailed with Paul. "Paul left the ship in Seattle and is on his way to Tokyo, or maybe Manila, I'm not sure. He asked me to give this envelope to you and tell you it might be six months before he gets back." Opal stared in disbelief.

"I think Paul sent you some money. I didn't open it. He told me not to. I'm honest, I don't need to steal from Paul or you. Well," he hesitated, "I might take some from Paul but only because he stole a couple hundred from me a year or so ago." Art laughed, then held out the envelope to Opal.

Opal slowly unlatched the door, opened it, and took the envelope. Anger was starting to boil. She looked at Art, and said, "That asshole left without telling me he wasn't coming back." She tore open the flap, and looked in the envelope: there was a small stack of fifty-dollar bills. More money than she had ever seen in her life. Slowly Opal folded over the torn flap of the envelope, then looked up at Art, standing there trying to be oblivious to Opal's situation.

"Mrs. Koenig, you don't know me. I'll only be in port another week, but if there's anything you need," he stopped and shifted his feet nervously. "Well, I been working around Paul a few years. He can be good sometimes, but I think he is just naturally mean. You married him, but I bet you didn't know him very well. I think he put his entire wages in that envelope, so don't cuss him out too much. I just don't think he is a one-woman man."

"He will be gone months," Opal said—a statement not a question. Her eyes went from the envelope to Art, then back to the envelope. "You like to come in for a cup of coffee? Just put some on to brew, and I'm baking." She opened the door further.

"Thanks, but no. Ship just got in and I haven't been home yet. I got myself a girl waiting for me, too. Kinda like to see her." His face flushed slightly as he lowered his eyes. "Opal, you got a job?" He looked over his shoulder as he started to turn away.

"No, Paul didn't want me to get a job. He said there were too many dangerous people out there." She looked down the street to the docks.

"Well, none of my business, but seems like you need something more than that to support yourself." He looked at the envelope in Opal's hand. "With the cost of things, that won't last all that long, figurin' you have to pay rent and groceries. I bet Paul didn't pay ahead six months on this place."

Opal, her anger at Paul still simmering, said softly, "no, he didn't and it probably won't." She wasn't worrying as much about paying for rent and food as she was about how she would spend the hours in each day.

"If I'm not stepping out of line, I think Frankie, my girl, might have a place for you to work. Her name is Francine but everyone calls her Frankie. She works with one of the ferry companies and they are always looking for help. I could ask her to come to talk to you. I think you two might hit it off. She's from here and has family and friends, but I know she probably gets lonely sometimes." Art looked down the street, then back to Opal. Their eyes met before Opal lowered hers.

Opal thought for a few seconds before answering. Her first impulse was to vent her anger on Paul's friend, but then, she wasn't sure how good a friend he was to Paul anyway. He was probably doing it more to help her than Paul. Opal stuttered, "Well, I guess. Yeah, maybe I will go get a job. Please tell Francine to stop by sometime. She sounds like a nice person. Yeah."

It was nearly a week before Opal met Francine, a willowy, smiling redhead. She was driving the same car Art had driven earlier. Francine explained that Art had left that morning for Seattle. "I don't like being alone but most of Art's trips are less than a month—and the pay is really good. We're saving to buy a house. Art hasn't proposed, but we're planning to get married before next spring."

Francine worked for the Bay Ferry Company. "It's owned by an Italian family with a good-looking son," she said. "I work in the office downtown, but they need help on the ferries in the coffee shops. Wages aren't great, but there are other jobs available with the company, too, and after awhile you should be able to get a better job." She paused. "Working conditions have improved a lot since the son returned from college back east and took over day-to-day management of his father's company."

The next Monday, Opal took a bus to the downtown offices of Bay Ferry Company. This was the first time she had been in the heart of the city. Up to then, Opal had spent her time in the apartment or in the immediate neighborhood, which had all the things she needed. Besides, she felt comfortable there, with working people as her neighbors. Being downtown was a totally new experience for her. The main offices were on the third floor, and she had forgotten to ask Francine which office she worked in. Opal walked up the stairs, embarrassed that she didn't know how to operate an elevator. She smiled to herself, "there aren't too many of these in Beaver County."

Opal had felt comfortable in her small hometown and had been seen as impetuous and never shy of taking charge of something. Here, she became painfully shy and nervous. Cautiously entering the main office, she was overwhelmed by the noise and activity—all the people and all the desks in the massive hall—and by not knowing who to talk to. A white-haired woman with a purple vest over a white blouse looked up at her and asked if she could help. Opal pulled out the piece of paper Francine had given her, on which she'd written: Billie Phillips—New Hires. Handing this to the woman, she stuttered, "Francine told me that I might find a job here." The woman smiled, pushed her chair away from her desk, and stood. "I'm Daisy Hance, I'll take you to see Mrs. Phillips. Please follow me."

Opal had never seen a building so big, much less walked down this long a hallway. They came to a door with a plaque that said Employment Office. Mrs. Hance opened the door and led Opal inside. Here, too, were rows of desks, with women sitting at typewriters, pulling folders out of filing cabinets, talking on telephones. Mrs. Hance and

Opal approached a middle-aged woman at a large desk piled with stacks of papers. The nameplate on the desk said, "Billie Phillips, New Hires."

Patting Opal's shoulder, Mrs. Hance said, "you'll be fine," and returned to her own office. Opal stood nervously waiting for Billie to end a telephone conversation. Billie motioned for Opal to sit, but she stood holding her handbag, nervously fingering the strap. Even having a handbag was new to Opal; she'd noticed most women had them, so she'd bought a cheap one. As Billie ended her phone conversation, she stood up to shake Opal's hand, and told her to have a seat. Opal sat down on the edge of the chair and cleared her throat.

"A friend said I might find a job here. She works for your company. Her name is Francine."

"Well, we are always looking for people." She asked Opal for her name, jotting it down on a slip of paper as Opal answered. "Before you tell me about yourself, let me tell you about our company."

She explained that the Bay Ferry Company ran more than ferries. They operated streetcars, a bus line to the small towns inland, and a garbage collection service. "This is why we have so many jobs—many of them are low-paying and hard work and it is a challenge keeping people." When she asked Opal what she had experience in, Opal looked at the floor and mumbled something inaudible.

"I'm sorry dear, I didn't hear you. Have you had a job before? You seem very young."

"I worked around the ranch. I can rope and ride a horse pretty good. I can cook some. I got married and came out here but my husband is a sailor and gone most of the time."

Billie smiled. "Well, unfortunately, we don't need many horse ropers or cow-girls. Can you type?" When Opal looked at her with a lost look in her eyes, Billie added, "Use a typewriter?" She looked down the row of desks at the women typing. Opal sighed and smiled, figuring her inexperience had already doomed her chances. "Guess I never even seen one before. I'm not used to the city. Guess I'm out of my place here." She started to get up.

"No, Opal, wait. Please sit." Billie reached over and put her hand on Opal's arm. Billie was very soothing and reassuring—she knew how to make someone feel comfortable.

Opal looked along the rows of desks and looking at Billie, she smiled again. "Except maybe the county fair, I guess I never seen so many people in one place." Opal's smile turned to a look of confusion, then she bit her lip as tears welled in her eyes. "I don't know what to do. Oh, I feel so helpless." She fumbled in her handbag for a non-existent handkerchief.

Billie pulled a freshly laundered hankie from a desk drawer and handed it to Opal. She stood, walked around her desk, pulled up a nearby chair and sat down next to Opal, putting her hand on Opal's arm. "Opal, I grew up on a farm east of here. The city can be scary. It took me several years to get used to all these people. But you know what, they are all just like you and me. We are all scared of something. You just have to wait until you feel comfortable with all the new things. It will come. I bet you are away from home for the first time aren't you?"

Opal nodded yes, then dabbed her eyes, shifting uneasily in her chair. Part of her wanted to get up and run as fast as she could, leaving behind this huge building. She was embarrassed and she was angry that Paul had made her humiliate herself like this. But Opal was proud and she did not know how to give up on anything. She thought about how she had fought back at school whenever anyone had made fun of her. She knew how to fight; she didn't know how to be scared.

Billie removed a sheet of paper from a stack on her desktop and laid it in front of Opal. "I want you to fill this out. We can find you a job. If you haven't done the type of work before, we will teach you. I have a feeling you are a quick learner and hard worker. I like that." She smiled. "And Opal, I like you. It took courage to come ask for a job. You fill this out and I will be back in a few minutes." She got up and walked between two rows of desks, stopping to talk to two of the typists at the far end.

Six

Two days later, Opal started work with the Bay Ferry Company—in the mailroom, mostly delivering mail, running errands, even cleaning the bathrooms. She was told that the job would be temporary until something else opened up. After a week, she started to enjoy the work. The pay wasn't very good, just like they told her, but she appreciated doing something she had never done before. It gave her confidence in meeting and talking to people. Several times, she had to leave the building and deliver packages to other businesses downtown. One day, she had to ride a company bus to Walnut Creek, several miles inland on the east side of the Berkeley Hills.

Dressed in her 'uniform' of white blouse, grey skirt, and purple vest with 'Bay Ferry Company' stitched on the chest pocket, her hair tied in a ponytail, Opal was showing the growing confidence she was gaining daily. She was proud to be identified with the bus line and feeling important when she handed the bus driver the card that allowed her to ride free. Of course, she was working for the company, but she felt important carrying the pouch marked with the company name.

She was seated next to a window on the trip back to Oakland, and a handsome young man, dressed casually, but very expensively, boarded at the last moment in Walnut Creek, and sat down next to her. He had dark hair, a trim mustache, and carried a leather briefcase. Opal was intimidated by his obvious importance, and pulled the pouch up against her and looked out the window. He nodded to her and pulled a notepad out of his briefcase. After he wrote down a few notes, he put it away and turned to her.

"Good afternoon. Are you enjoying this nice day?"

"Oh yes, I had to take some things to Walnut Creek. It's nice to get out of the office."

"Do you work in Oakland?"

"Yes, I just started recently. I work in the mailroom, but they said I could work my way up if I wanted."

The man looked intensely at her. "Do you want to work your way up?" As she fidgeted in the seat, he smiled.

"Oh yes. The company is good and cares for us workers. A lot of people have told me that." She looked down at her almost empty pouch and re-tied the string closure.

"What would you like to do? I hear they have a lot of different jobs."

Opal looked up at his tanned face. He had a slight foreign accent. She thought it European but hadn't had enough contact with foreigners to be sure. "I've never been on the ocean. I'd like to work on the ferries."

"What makes you think you would like being on the water? Some people get seasick, even though it's only a few minutes across the Bay."

"My husband is in the merchant marine, so he is gone most of the time. He loves the sea." Opal trailed off as she said, the sea.

"My goodness, you don't look old enough to be married. You must be a newlywed. Are you from the Bay Area?"

"Oh no. I'm from Colorado. I only got married a few months ago. My husband sails from here so we moved out here."

"So you are working to stay busy. And earn a little money," the man smiled as he said this. "What is your name?"

"Opal. And you are?"

"Alberto. I am glad to meet you, Opal."

~

This was the first meeting of Opal and the son of the owner of the Bay Ferry Company. He didn't tell her anything about himself other than his first name. She had no idea he was her boss, and the boss of hundreds of other people. On that trip back to the city, they chatted about California, Colorado, the ocean, and many other little things. Opal was usually shy around strangers, but she felt comfortable talking with Alberto. He learned much about her but kept details of who he was to himself. She was too shy to ask, still thinking he must be someone important.

A week later, Billie called Opal to her desk. Afraid she had done something wrong, Opal approached with her head down. Billie laughed and asked Opal what she had done. Sure that she was about to be fired, Opal shook her head and said weakly she didn't know, she was trying to work hard.

"Well Opal, you must have impressed the big boss because I got a note from him this morning re-assigning you to one of the ferries. That doesn't happen very often. A note from the boss, that is."

Opal's eyes were wide open as she stuttered, "I don't know the boss. How can he know me?"

Billie handed the note to Opal. Written in very elegant handwriting was the order, signed by Alberto.

Opal threw her hands to her mouth, stifling a sharp intake of air. "Alberto? Alberto? Does he have dark hair and a mustache?"

"Well, yes, I would say. I would also say one of the handsomest men in the Bay Area. You have never met him? I see him in the building on most days. Maybe you have delivered mail to him?"

Opal stared at Billie, hands still to her mouth. She looked around at the rows of desks in the large room. "He did this for me? He was so nice to me. I only met him once. On the bus. He was riding his own bus. He owns the bus." Opal continued to mouth words, but there was no sound.

Billie laughed as she reached over and took back the note. "Whatever you said or did, you impressed the boss. Congratulations! Tomorrow, you report for work at the docks. Go downstairs right now to the laundry and pick up your new uniform. They will sew your first name on the vest pocket."

Feeling like she was floating on air as she returned to the mail room, Opal—for the first time in her life—felt like someone important. She had been made fun of, abused by her father, taken advantage of by her mother and siblings, forever made to feel inferior—growing up in a place and time that did not value girls or women other than for their ability to serve men. Now she was doing something on her own—living basically by herself, learning steadily that marrying Paul was a huge mistake. Alberto was the first man to treat her like she was important; at first, intimidated by him, but now she was intrigued. "He's very good-looking," she sighed to herself.

Opal started work as a ticket taker on the *Sea Lion* ferry, running six round trips a day between Oakland and the pier next to the Ferry Building in San Francisco. She loved the Bay and always brought bread crumbs to throw to the seagulls. On her first day, Alberto rode the third ferry to the City. He smiled as he shook hands with his new ticket-girl. He told her she looked very nice, but he diplomatically handed her a card for a beautician he said he asked all his girls to visit. "Thelma will help you with grooming tips. She makes all the girls look like Sirens." Opal didn't know what that meant, but she assumed Alberto wanted his ferry girls to all look alike. She certainly didn't think herself pretty, but maybe she could look nicer for Paul, whenever he came home. Maybe he would treat her better if she was beautiful. She hadn't heard from Paul for weeks, but that didn't bother her. Yet.

~

Two weeks later, Paul staggered into the apartment during the middle of the day, and Opal wasn't there. When she came home from her long day at work, Paul angrily asked her where she'd been. After she excitedly told him about her new job, he viciously slapped her face. He told her in a drunken slur that no wife of his was going to work. When Opal burst into tears and ran into the bedroom and locked the door, Paul stumbled out of the apartment and found his way to another bar. The swelling and bruising on her face were so severe, Opal had to call in sick for the next four days. Paul came and went, and when he sobered up on his third day home, he apologized to her and said she could work, but he still didn't like it. He was scheduled to be home for a month, but after another week, he suddenly left. His note to Opal when she got home from work a rainy Wednesday night simply said, "Gone to Tokyo. Back in a month or so." The rent was due in a week, but he'd left her no money for that or for food.

Opal's appointments with Thelma and her growing friendship with Francine had increased her self-confidence but she was embarrassed to talk with Francine about Paul. Alberto was riding the ferry almost every other day, and was shocked to see Opal on her first day at work after her 'sickness.' She had bruises on her left hand and wrist and a scab on her right cheek. She made excuses, but when the perceptive Alberto started asking her questions, she broke down and told him that her husband had come home and hit her. Alberto started checking with the shipping companies and learned more than he wanted to about Paul: he'd been fired from two companies for drinking and fighting; they usually had to bail him out of jail in the ports around the Pacific; he fought on board. Alberto had seen this type of behavior before, and did not tolerate anyone like Paul working for him. He took pity on Opal—liked her and tried to counsel her—but knew he had to be careful. She was a confused girl away from home—with lots of promise—but stubborn and too proud to admit her mistake in marrying Paul.

Opal was doing a good job on the ferry, and able to forget her troubled home life while at work. Paul came into port three times in the next six months. Each time, Opal called in sick. Alberto wanted to call the police but was hesitant to get involved with an employee. Even so, he started to spend more time with Opal, both at work and on several evenings. He rationalized that while she was making decent wages, the pay for female employees was not meant to be career wages. Most of the company's female employees were either married or living with their parents. He knew Opal was struggling to make ends meet. So, every Tuesday evening he took her to dinner in the City. Against all his instincts, he was falling for her. He didn't know how much was pity and how much was romance. He was rich, good-looking, powerful; he could have any woman in the Bay Area—but was falling in love with this simple country girl. This married girl, although in his eyes, the marriage was a sham. It was obvious Opal was trapped and couldn't get out. He had seen Opal gain strength and self-confidence in the months she worked for his company, but whenever Paul was home, she became withdrawn, like a wounded animal.

Wisely, Alberto arranged for Opal to get a job as assistant to a close friend who was vice-president of the Board of Trustees for the Golden Gate Children's Hospital Foundation. Alberto wanted her out of his own company, away from any implications of romancing an employee. Although the job took her away from the ferry and the company that she had grown to like, Opal's salary doubled. Her new employer recognized—as Mrs. Phillips had—that Opal was a fast and eager learner and she quickly mastered the skills necessary to engage with people to convince them to donate money to the foundation. She continued living in the apartment down by the docks, but when she went another four months without hearing from Paul, she moved to a nicer apartment near the university in Berkeley.

Alberto started seeing her on strictly social occasions, taking her regularly to San Francisco. He borrowed a sailboat from an uncle and took her sailing through the Golden Gate and north along the coast.

He bought her nice clothes, including jewelry which she was not even sure how to wear. When he asked her if she enjoyed opera, she laughed and said she didn't even know what it was. Her first visit to the San Francisco Opera House was for Puccini's *Madame Butterfly*. She whispered to Alberto that she couldn't understand what they were saying, so he unobtrusively translated from his native Italian every word said and sung.

One night two months later, Alberto said he had gotten tickets to the new Puccini opera—*Turandot*—which was opening in San Francisco. By then, Opal had seen a half dozen operas, three by Puccini. She was starting to like Puccini, but mostly because it made her think of Alberto. This was all so new to Opal. Her world was expanding exponentially. When the big evening came, he gave Opal a new gown and pearl necklace. As they came into the Opera House, a photographer took their picture. Opal showed a new side to her with her elegant look. Alberto had sent her to Thelma, who arranged her hair and did her eyes, nails, even toenails. As Opal stood next to this handsome man, she glowed for the camera. After the performance, they spent the night in a room at the Mark Hopkins. Opal made one of the arias from *Turandot* 'her and Alberto's' song: "Nessun Dorma"—never sleeps. She and Alberto laughed about it—they didn't sleep that night as they discovered new wonders about each other in the elegant setting of the Mark.

When Opal returned to her new apartment the next morning, Paul was sitting on the steps. "It took me two days to find you!" He hit her as he told her to let him into the apartment. She told him she was in love with another man and wanted a divorce. "You're never home and when you are, you beat me—I'm a new woman and will not stand for this!" In the privacy of the apartment, he hit her so hard he knocked her against the wall. Then he ripped off her new gown and threw it in the garbage and forced her to tell him about Alberto. In the chaos of those moments Paul didn't notice the Turandot 78 as it slipped behind the davenport, unbroken.

Three days later—while Paul was down at the docks—Opal saw the front page of the *Oakland Tribune* describing the tragic car wreck that had killed the head of the Bay Ferry Company. As Alberto drove down the curving road from his Berkeley Hills mansion, the brakes had failed, sending his Kissel Speedster off a steep hill and crashing into a tree, killing him instantly.

Stunned by the news, Opal guessed that Paul was responsible. Fearing for her own safety, she called Francine to tell her she was leaving Oakland in a hurry, and asked her to come by the apartment later and collect her few possessions—including the *Turandot*, two other Puccini 78s, and the photo at the opera that had been delivered by messenger a day earlier while Paul was out. As Opal was then preparing to call the police, Paul returned, bound her hands and gagged her, put her in his car, started driving and didn't stop until reaching Long Beach. He had a new job at the docks there. Opal was his wife and he demanded she serve him. He beat and raped her repeatedly, and though she did not know it at the time, gave her diseases that would impact the rest of her life.

All the respect and pride Opal had gained over the past two years was destroyed. She could not escape Paul. He did not sail anywhere, working at the docks instead. She had become pregnant but lost the baby soon after arriving in southern California. She knew the miscarriage was due to his beatings. The resulting surgery to repair the damage from the beatings left a scar she pointed to in later years as what Paul did to her, along with the knife scars on her breast where Paul cut her in one of his drunken rages. Her life turned into a long nightmare. It ended one day when he returned to the tiny apartment near the docks sober for a change, and said he had a new job that would take him to Asia. He shipped out immediately, as he had in Oakland, but this time—sober and slightly repentant—he left her a little money, which she used to buy herself new clothes, something he had denied her. And she treated herself to a bus ride to Huntington Beach occasionally to sit in the sand and let the ocean breezes soothe her battered soul. She didn't have the confidence anymore to try and get to know anyone. She had let her looks go and was always afraid of what Paul might do when he came back. Being half a world away didn't seem to matter. After Paul had been gone for two months, she found a waitressing job at a small restaurant within walking distance of the apartment; the wages and tips were sufficient for rent, and meals came with the job.

Opal did not know or understand about battered wives. She did not dare to leave and would not report any of this to the police. Something had been taken out of her after Alberto's death, and whenever Opal had gained a little courage, Paul had beat it out of her.

A year later, on a rainy April night, she answered a knock at her door. It was a gentleman from the shipping company. He told her Paul had been killed in Singapore. The details were sketchy, but evidently he had gotten drunk, tried to rob some locals, and was knifed. His body was thrown into the bay, and found two days later by the harbor police. The gentleman gave her the duffle with Paul's few belongings and handed her a check for $1500: Paul's wages plus the payout from a small insurance policy the company carried.

She was now free from the man she hated and despised, but had not been able to get away from. She was also free from the man she loved, but who had been murdered by her husband. Lost, scared, beaten—she was barely capable of dealing with anything anymore—she just wanted to go home. She could never call California home. It reminded her of Paul, but more tragically, it reminded her of Alberto.

Opal rode the bus to Huntington Beach one last time, to sit in the sand and watch the waves and gulls—and sort out in her mind what she needed to do to get home to Beaver Creek. First of all: call Francine to ship to her the few things she had left in the Oakland apartment; these included three 78 rpm Puccini records and the photograph of her and Alberto in front of the San Francisco Opera. Then, give notice at the restaurant and to the landlord. Then, make train reservations. Then pack.

On a bright sunny morning, Opal boarded the train heading east. Her trip across the California and Nevada and Utah deserts seemed to take forever. She was thinking of a dark, laughing young Italian named Alberto as she saw the endless miles of sagebrush go by.

~

Opal shook her head and rubbed her eyes, and realized the bright sunny sky was in Colorado and the land was hers—all hers. Instead of a chipmunk scolding her from a nearby tree, a scrub jay was noisily complaining about the sun being low in the western sky. Clouds were drifting in, beginning to obscure the sun, the breeze was picking up. "Must be a storm coming," she told the jay.

"What has happened to me?" She thought of her transformation under Alberto's guidance—a beautiful, confident young woman, with a job of her own, dealing with wealthy and important people. She'd had a bright future. It was a dream come true—more than a dream, since she had never anticipated anything like that. Then it was over—the dream become a nightmare.

No one knew she had become pregnant in California, and lost the baby in a miscarriage. Nor of the diseases her husband brought to her as gifts from his reckless world-whoring sprees, resulting in a hysterectomy that left her unable to be a mother. The diseases would do more than deprive her of motherhood. They would deprive her of a normal body and brain.

Some days Opal felt broken—hope and confidence gone, no ambition, no drive, no desire. Living in a log cabin, sharing it with a drifter of a man. Spending her days minding chickens and pigs and goats, mending fences, chopping firewood. She would sit on the porch, listening and rocking, and stare across the valley to the distant San Juans. She saw the expanse of the valley as ocean. The snowcapped peaks made her think of the Sierra but were as inaccessible to her as was Alberto.

The jay complained once more, then flew off with the wind. There was no ocean, there were no seagulls, no ferries, no Alberto. "All I have are the Puccini records that I still have trouble understanding. But—I own this piece of mesa, with trees, and ravens, and chipmunks!"

Seven

DAILY LIFE SETTLED INTO routines with little variation. The hard times of the Depression were over, the second big war was over. But life on Bean Ridge was never easy. A few more people were living on the mesa—life still was a mixture of ranching, working in the orchards, living off the land. Ranches large and small were being subdivided: rocky soil and scarce water made living off the land challenging. Deer numbers were increasing from the lows in previous decades; elk were wandering through snow-covered pastures; and winters didn't seem to be as long or as harsh. Roads still were not paved and the winter and spring mud kept vehicle traffic difficult, especially coming up and down the grades onto and off the mesa.

Stimulated by FDR's New Deal rural electrification program, the local electric company brought a line up through Opal's east forty acres and north along her lane easement, including the rights to have a primitive road along the line. Opal had grown up without electricity, and became accustomed to having it in California. In the years since returning to Beaver County, she lived without it, but now she could have lights at night and maybe splurge on an icebox and a record player she didn't have to hand crank.

Opal never really understood the legalities of this easement and often would run linemen off with a shotgun. After awhile, meter readers refused to come onto her property to read her meter. They knew about how much she would use, which wasn't much, and billed accordingly, but they still needed to access the line for repairs. Several times, they had the Sheriff accompany them, but they often walked up from below and made their repairs and secretly eased back off the property without her seeing them.

The documents involving the electric line easement used her legal name: Koenig—Opal Koenig, widow of Paul Koenig. The thought repulsed her. Her mother once commented on Willy being her common-law husband. Opal didn't understand what that meant, but she vowed to herself she would never again utter that vile name, Koenig.

So she became Opal Long. Since she didn't go out into the civilized world very often and didn't relate to people or legal things, she thought it wouldn't make any difference. In the intervening years, Opal Long finally erased the last lingering association with her husband. Whatever Willy was, no piece of paper called him her husband.

Willy didn't hang around the cabin doing nothing—or even near it—any time of year. Opal learned the secret of getting him out of sight whenever he started to drive her crazy with his puttering around: pull out the record player, take a Puccini record out of its cover, and put it on the turntable. If Willy didn't see her do that, then he certainly heard it once it started playing. It took him no time to either grab his jacket or grab his truck keys. He never said anything to Opal, but the truth was he often found Opal intolerable to be around. Her depression or apathy made him uncomfortable. And Opal didn't say anything to Willy, but the truth was she often found him intolerable as well. Regardless, the relationship seemed to work, but neither understood why.

Willy seemed industrious at times, especially noticeable as his 'junk' expanded to cover the west-facing hillside next to the cabin. He was not good at mechanical repair, but people learned that if they needed a part, Willy might be the one to have what they needed. Although he rarely paid for the junk he hauled in, he certainly charged someone if they found a part they needed. He also used truck, auto, woodstove, and bed frame parts around the property: a rectangular, hinged pair of Model A Ford windows was perfect in the southwest corner of the cabin; the folding bonnet hood of an early Oldsmobile became part of the root cellar roof; a Chevy pickup door (passenger side) was just right for a gate on one of the goat enclosures.

Opal and the goats were often at war, especially in her flower and vegetable gardens. She was proud of the dark blue irises and the Bouncing Bets that Della had shared with her, and the lilacs and roses Willy brought one April late in the Depression. He had pulled his truck up to the cabin back door and honked the horn. Opal had been taking a nap, so was not pleased with the intrusion. She stumbled out, thinking there was a problem, but Willy leaned out the driver's side window and grinned. She had come to recognize the grin as his way of expecting thanks for some little favor he did or was about to do. As always, she told him he was acting like a little kid, but that made him grin even wider.

"Look in the back of the truck for what I got you. Where do you want 'em?"

"Oh Lord, Willy, what did you steal now?" She stared at him but knew she would get no explanation until she walked back there to look. Sometimes she would come eye-to-eye with piglets, or blind chickens, or one time a road-killed deer. With a frown on her face, she walked to the back and looked in.

"A truckload of dirt. Willy, we got all we want right here."

"No, woman, it's plants." He got out and walked back and stood beside her. "Oh, looks like they got covered up." He laughed as he dug through the pile of soil. Twigs and leaves emerged. "You like lilacs don't you? Well, I got some lilac twigs. And two kinds of yeller roses back here," he said as he exposed more plants. "Guess they got all buried up on the rough road down there. Got the roots with 'em all."

"You sure didn't buy them. Where'd you steal them?"

"I don't steal. You know that. The Albertsons sold their place down by the river. Bert told me before he left that I could take some plants if I wanted them. New owners ain't there yet. They paid for the house, not the plants. They won't know any is gone. I only took a few on the edges. Even filled in the holes. I wanted you to have something pretty."

Opal had to smile. She knew Willy meant well and had a heart as big as the mesa. Even though he would take what was not his without any qualms, he was just as easy to give back when someone was in need— generous as the winter air was cold after a storm. Easy come, easy go was his motto. Willy irritated the hell out of her more often than not, but she could never stay mad at him. "How can I get mad at you, you silly old fart? Where do we put them?"

"Don't look at me. You are the gardener. You put them where you want. You dig the holes and I will put them in."

"No, you got that backward. You dig the holes and I will sort through this mess you have and I will plant them. You don't know how to plant anything." Opal laughed and grinned at him, "I'm not even sure you know how to use a shovel."

Willy shot back, "Who dug your root cellar? Do you think I tamed a badger to dig that? Don't know how to use a shovel? I'll be the one to dig your grave, woman. You be nice to me or I'll take these back to where I got them."

Opal walked around for a few minutes talking to herself. "Here. Lilac right here." She picked up a rock and set it there. "Dig down about a foot. They will get the tailwater here so we won't have to water them. I'll see it right out the window when I first wake up. That will certainly be prettier than your ugly face." Her laugh had turned into more of a cackle nowadays. She wandered around some more, putting a rock or stick in different places. Willy pulled the shovel from the truck bed, leaned on it, and watched her, becoming concerned over the number of holes he was going to have to dig.

"Don't just stand there gawking. Start pulling out the plants. I don't know how many you got."

"Damnation, I wouldn't have dug so many if I knew I had to plant them!"

"You don't have to plant them. I don't want you to plant them. I want you to dig the holes. You dug them out of the ground. I'll put them in. You just dig me a hole to put them in. You wanted me to have all these. Let's get to work."

The four groups of lilacs each contained three or four starts. She made three major clumps of roses, each with about five starts. She was impressed that Willy had dug up so many. He was complaining of blisters by the time he finished digging. He was complaining that he had even more after she made him haul water up from the creek to water them—unfortunately it was too early for the tailwater.

It all paid off. By the third spring, all of the starts had prospered and were rapidly growing. The roses took off and were spreading; Opal had planted these next to the cabin and within five years, they nearly obscured the west side. The lilacs were in the flower garden area and stayed within their clumps. She stretched chicken wire around them the first several years to keep the goats out; the goats ate new lilac shoots that grew outside the wire, but they couldn't keep up with the roses, which seemed to spread even more as the goats trimmed them back.

The silver poplars grew taller and larger around, and the tailwater was sufficient for all her plants once they were established. Opal enjoyed digging trenches to channel the water through the garden and flowers. It gave her results and as long as she saw the benefits of it, she didn't mind the labor. Of course, Willy often headed for the truck when he saw her pick up the shovel, but didn't hesitate to eat the potatoes or beans from the garden. Her old standbys—chicken wire, boards, hog wire, and auto and truck parts—served as adequate fencing for the garden. That, plus constant rock-throwing, kept the goats away at least enough to let the vegetables grow and mature.

During a dry year in the early '50s, tailwater was sparse. Willy drove up one July afternoon and honked. Opal had been canning cherries, sweating over the hot stove in the cabin. She was glad to take a break but knew the meaning of the honking: Willy had a new appropriation to show her. "What'd you drag home now, old man?"

"I got me a water pump. Works. We can tote it down to the creek and build up the rock barrier that old man Sampson built years ago across the creek. I can get some pipe and electric wire. We can pump water up here whenever we don't get the tailwater. Maybe even put in plumbing where you can take a bath."

"The day that happens is the day you throw dirt on my grave. You were wrong when you said 'we' can do all that. I'm sure you meant to say 'I' can do all that."

But together they managed to get the pump down the hill, and as Opal correctly guessed, they put in many hours piling rocks on the crude dam to pond water behind it. Within a week, Willy brought home a few hundred feet of new plastic pipe and heavy-duty electrical wire. Opal rolled her eyes when he said it had fallen off a truck and was just lying alongside the river road. They soon had water pumping uphill, although they spent more time repairing split pipe or loose connections than enjoying flowing water. But it served in a pinch. Opal never did get a bathroom or anything resembling indoor plumbing.

Opal didn't think it a good idea to drink the water since the animals drank from the ponds, but that didn't stop Willy. Several times he got violently ill, with severe diarrhea, but he didn't believe Opal when she blamed it on the water. He said he drank out of creeks and streams all his life and his stomach could handle it. She laughed when she told him she didn't think so.

Willy never ceased to amaze Opal. Every once in a while, he would come struggling up the hill dragging a juniper post. He didn't steal everything they used. One thing they had plenty of was rocks and juniper trees. Some of the trees had been cut years before they moved here. Willy marveled that someone would walk all the way down to the creek over steep and rocky deer trails and cut a tree, or even a large branch and drag it up top when there were dozens, even hundreds of good post trees on top already. But he also realized the taller, straighter trees were down near the water. If they needed a straight post, tall enough to function, he had to go downhill to cut one, limb it, and drag it up the hillside. (After the Sheriff caught him several times, Willy became gun shy of stealing posts.)

Over time, Opal had become unconcerned over Willy's lack of morals, coming to get a kick out of his antics. Everyone else on the mesa had more concern than she did, and she used twisted logic to justify it.

Like the day Opal heard lambs bleating outside her door. Of course, she immediately hollered for Willy, to chastise him for stealing them. When he came up the hill—from doing what, she had no idea—he shook his head and told her that, no, he did not steal these two little guys, that they wandered onto the place on their own. Opal had noticed a flock being trailed along the road the day before, so, yes, maybe the lambs had gotten separated and made it to their place. Maybe they latched onto one of her goats, thinking it would suffice for a new mama.

"Willy, you need to go find the flock and herder and return these lambs to where they belong."

Willy made his frowny 'I beg your pardon' look and spit out his wad of tobacco. "Now look here woman, you need to think this through. These are a gift to us. No one will ever notice these guys are missing. Do you know how many sheep were in that flock that went by yesterday? Must be at least a thousand. They're up on the mountain by now and probably a half dozen lambs been eaten by a bear or lion already. Besides, you know how many flocks are up there?" He pointed to the mountains with his head. "Dozens. Who knows where their mommas are now."

"I'm sure you could find out if you thought you would get a reward."

"You are still not thinking straight. They don't miss these two. The rich owners don't care. Now think what we can do with them." He looked closely underneath the two lambs, now slowly grazing Opal's flower beds. "A little boy and a little girl. Maybe you don't remember about this type of thing, but a boy and a girl can make a few more boys and girls. And they can make a few more. Pretty soon, we got mutton, fresh lamb meat, and enough wool to make me a new coat."

"You gonna shoot the coyotes that come prowling every night? You gonna tie them up to keep them from going right back through that sorry line of sagging wire you call a fence?"

"I have been thinking of puttin' in some cross fencing to keep the goats where we need them. They spend too much time in your flowers anyway."

Opal looked at Willy, then threw a rock to shoo the lambs from the lilac bushes. "Tarnation old man, but damned if you don't make some sense once in a blue moon."

The lambs somehow survived two months before a coyote took the female. But that was motivation enough for Willy to string a few hundred yards of barbed wire fence over on the east ridge. Even Opal knew a two-strand barbed wire fence would not hold a goat or a lamb, but she enjoyed Willy producing something with potential usefulness. And with some tinkering, she might make it strong enough to keep the goats out of her flowers. She would just use chicken wire from Willy's junkyard on the garden fence to goat-proof it.

~

People on Bean Ridge were very self-sufficient and Opal and Willy followed that trend. During the long winters at this 6500-foot elevation mesa, the dirt roads became almost impassable. Until the late Fifties, few people needed to drive into town very often. There were no commuters, and 'going-to-town' days could be postponed for days at a time. Even until the Eisenhower years, there were as many mules and wagons on the roads as automobiles. There were two one-room schools on the mesa. Students rode horses to school and many walked. And it was a community effort to hook a large log to a workhorse and drag a path along a road so the kids could reach school when snow was deep, which it often was. In addition the spring melt and summer thunderstorms made roads muddy bogs.

Even though the residents of the mesa were isolated, most of them made efforts to get together for dances, socials, and picnics, usually at the schools. All except Opal and Willy. As a result, they were often the subjects of whispers and gossip. No one really knew these two outcasts and loners who lived on the edge of the mesa, out of sight of the rest of the community.

Opal realized she was surviving quite comfortably—well, 'comfortably' in a very loose relative way—but she also understood what she had given up. Since she had basically become a recluse, she didn't associate with people other than Willy, and sometimes she wondered if he counted as people. But if she had been even a bit social, she likely would have heard the gossip and discussions about her. Her neighbors—who seldom saw her—called her the goat lady, a witch, that crazy old woman. She wouldn't have cared; although, in rare moments of reflection, she thought that she should care. Besides, she wasn't old. Or at least as old as she looked. Maybe that was why she avoided looking in mirrors.

Less and less frequently she wondered, "What happened to that lady standing outside the opera?" She would occasionally pull out the photograph of her and Alberto; for the first few years, a tear would run down her cheek when she relived the memories. "That wasn't me," she would think. "I belong here. Maybe I would like a bathtub once in a while," she mused. But she accepted that would never happen either. She was like the deer and the coyotes; real life meant freedom to be what she wanted to be. Well, freedom to be.

~

Her situation suited Opal. The cabin was a half-mile from the road, although she rarely ventured out to it. She was on the edge of settlement, so she would never have any close neighbors. The lay of the land guaranteed that, since everything was downhill on three sides—steep, rocky, and filled with junipers and sagebrush. Opal did enjoy sitting on her porch and staring off at the view, which seemed to change morning-to-night, season-to-season. Over the years, she noticed more and more buildings and lights down in the valley. She often smiled at the thought that they were all down there and she was up in her secret spot. She grew to appreciate the isolation. She was far enough off the road so nothing was visible that indicated there was anything or anyone on her property.

Opal chose this existence, though she still occasionally missed the life that whirled around without her, the world she had cast aside. But as the years went by, she continued losing touch with the changes and the technology that improved so many other lives. Willy interacted with that world, but Opal became more and more reclusive. World events passed her by as well as many other things. She didn't vote. Hell, she barely knew who was president. What did it matter to her, anyway? Through Willy, through occasional newspapers and magazines, and by chance encounters with customers who came to barter with Willy for car parts (or to retrieve 'borrowed' items) she knew enough to realize she was better off here.

Having never thought of her home and the land as an investment, Opal made no efforts to do anything that might increase its value. It would be home until she died, so it didn't matter that a better lane or better fences or a general clean-up of the property would be good things to do. Those things cost money, which she did not have. Even though there now was a county dump, her hillsides were much easier for disposal of things unwanted. And she had plenty of hillsides and plenty of unwanted old cans, jars, car parts, wire, boards, nails. The hillside out her east door became the junkyard. Somewhere along the way, Opal quit thinking of her place as a beautiful natural forest and turned it into a garbage dump. If she didn't care, why should anyone else?

In the early years, she had occasionally wondered what she might be doing if things had turned out differently and she had stayed in the Bay area (married to Alberto, raising children, an executive to a corporate president, a community leader). But whenever those thoughts crossed her mind, the face of Paul came into the picture, as did the body of Alberto murdered because of her and her bad choice of a husband. Maybe she was not able to make good choices; maybe she really did belong up here isolated where bad choices didn't affect anyone else. Over time those maybes and what-ifs faded and disappeared into the sage and juniper hillsides, flowing away from her like the water in the spring-fed creeks.

Eight

OVER THE YEARS THAD'S health declined, due to a combination of working in West Virginia coal mines as a young man, and the dusty air typical of Colorado ranching. As he became more and more an invalid, Della needed someone to talk to, even if it was Opal, since Eugene, Rand and Dinah had all moved away. Della would occasionally drive Thad's old truck up the hill to Bean Ridge and visit her. Telephone lines ran alongside the main road and Della made arrangements for the phone company to run a line down Opal's lane to her cabin; one day Della took Opal to see Thad and had the phone workers hastily run the line. When Opal returned with Della, she had a telephone.

Della taught Opal how to use the phone, particularly which ring on the 5-party line was hers, but Opal couldn't understand that three shorts and one long was the only time she was to answer the phone. It didn't take long for the neighbors to realize that whenever the phone would ring—whether it be three short and one long, two long and one short or the other three combinations—Opal would answer, then swear like a sailor when they told her it wasn't for her. She was confused when someone would tell her to hang up, and her hearing was starting to fade so she would almost yell into the phone. Since Della was the only one who called Opal, they settled on a call at 8 a.m. and another at 8 p.m.; amazingly she convinced Opal she shouldn't answer a call at any other time.

Willy would occasionally call someone but Opal rarely did. He would hightail it away from the cabin whenever Opal and Della talked. Opal would yell, ask questions, and argue. They spent much time talking about mundane things, and Opal always complained about things Willy did, or more often, didn't do. This was troubling for him, since, after every phone call or visit by Della, Opal would light into him for some character flaw or performance failure.

Willy thought it would be funny if it wasn't so obnoxious. If he could comment from Heaven, or wherever he may end up, he would say his death was hastened by Opal's phone conversations with her mother and her constant playing of the Puccini records. He came close on several occasions to packing up and leaving but always thought better of it: where else could he get taken care of like he did? So he put up with the abuse.

~

Not long after Thad died, Della moved in with Abe Conger, a widowed rancher who lived a mile north of Opal. Thad's ranch wasn't worth much, so there was very little for Della to inherit, and she had to sell the ranch to pay taxes. It was too small to be a viable operation anymore; the neighbor who bought it burned the old house and added the acreage to his existing ranch.

Back in those days, part of looking after yourself in this subsistence lifestyle was to team up with somebody in the same situation. Abe had lost his wife to cancer and was struggling to live alone. He was busy in the fields and with the livestock all day and had no time or interest in cooking, cleaning or laundry. So Della moved in and helped put her life and Abe's back together. Now living near Opal, she naturally spent more time with her unusual daughter. Her other children had scattered out of the valley, as many young people tended to do. Della's life had been raising children, keeping other people productive and whole; she couldn't think of any other way to spend her time than to continue what she knew how to do.

And she knew her daughter was troubled—that Opal was coping the only way she knew how—by retreating to the homestead and shutting out the world. Opal did not fit with normal society, and Willy, well, he was Willy; together, both seemed to flutter around the edges of civilization.

Two or three times a week, Della would saddle Abe's jack mule, and ride cross-country to Opal's place. Abe needed his pickup most of the time and the distance was just a tad too far to walk for her arthritic knees.

To give her mother a place to sleep when she spent the night—when Abe was hunting or off buying or selling cows or sheep—Opal gave Ma her room. The few possessions she treasured, such as the photograph of her and Alberto, the Puccini records and record player—were kept in that room. She hid her remaining jar of silver and gold coins in the bottom drawer of the bureau; by this time, Opal had forgotten about the jar of gold coins she buried years ago. She moved her own bed into the back room off the kitchen, and moved Willy's bed from there to the enclosed front porch. Willy complained until he was blue but it did no good. His only other option was to sleep outside (which he did in decent weather), or build another small cabin or room of his own. He thought about it for a few minutes and decided that was too much trouble. Besides, the cats slept with him half the time and they could help keep him warm.

Since Willy and Della did not get along, he disappeared whenever Della visited. Della's room became just that—her room—and she spent a lot of time in it, often with Opal and with the door closed. The door stayed closed when she wasn't there and Willy learned quickly that no one—meaning him—was to go in there. He tried to sneak a peek once when Della was not there, but Opal caught him and banished him for a week. There was nothing special in it that he knew of, but he figured Opal must have gotten some of her strangeness from her mother and the two of them together was more than he could deal with. He prayed (or whatever resembled praying in his world) that Della would never move in permanently—that would be the end of him.

As Della became more frail, her visits tapered off. Sometimes Opal would walk north through the fields to Della's. She didn't feel comfortable walking where people could see her, so she avoided the roads. Once when she crossed the Simpson's field, old man Simpson yelled at her to stay off his property; she had run him off with a shotgun once when he came down to visit Willy, so he figured it was fair play. She quit her visits to Ma after that.

One January morning when she called her mother, Abe answered the phone and told her that Della had passed away in her sleep. Opal didn't go to the funeral; she figured that part of her life was over. She had relied on her mother to be the one person from her past life she could talk to, yet she still blamed Ma for a lot of her troubles. Besides, she didn't want to dress up (as if she had anything decent to wear) and go out in public.

~

Opal's half-brother and his family had been living in California for several years. Rand was never close to his half-sister; after all, she was almost 20 years older than him. And his wife Annie and two young daughters had never met Opal. They had recently moved to the Ridge and lived only two miles away. At her mother-in-law's funeral, Annie asked family members where Opal was. She heard numerous comments about Della's strange daughter, including that Della and Opal were a pair cut from the same cloth.

The day after the funeral, Annie summoned up her courage and drove to Opal's—successfully navigating the half-mile long track. When she got to the cabin, no one was there. She found this strange, hearing that Opal rarely left the property. As she was looking around outside the cabin, mildly horrified at its appearance, she heard a yell from down by the creek. She turned and saw an unshaven, partly bald, overweight man come puffing up the hill. A woman—dressed as sloppily as him—was scrambling up the hill, too, throwing rocks and old cans at him.

Annie chuckled at the sight, although she was a little frightened they both might take after her.

"You worthless old bum. You knew the pump had fallen in the pond. Now it's ruined and how will we get any water? You gonna haul it up this hill? One more trip up and we will be burying you."

"Tarnation, you crazy woman. Quit throwing things at me. How was I to know the goats had gotten out of the fence? They want to drink too."

"You call that a fence? A goat wouldn't even know it stepped over that worthless piece of wire."

"Nothing to keep you from mending it yourself. If you would water them critters then they wouldn't go searching for water."

"What do I water them with? There is no water on top of the hill. If you were smart, you would know water don't run uphill. You don't do anything else around..." Opal stopped as she neared the cabin and saw the strange car. "Who are you?" She yelled at the woman on the cabin porch. "Who are you? You are trespassing. I'll get my shotgun."

Annie stepped off the porch and held out her hands. "Hi, Opal. I am your sister-in-law, Annie. I wanted to stop by and say hello and say how sorry I am about your mother."

Opal staggered up to the porch as Willy disappeared behind the outhouse and made his way toward the garden.

"Who? Annie who? I don't got no sister-in-law. Which brother? All of 'em are worthless and never have bothered to say nothin' to me."

In that moment, Annie knew first hand that all the stories and gossip were true: this woman was one of a kind. And the old man with her? Well, she soon learned he and Opal went together. But that would end when this old man was gone, which by his wheezing and breathing, sounded sooner than later. Then, Opal would be truly alone. Annie screwed up her courage and determination—and her religious convictions to help others—and decided she would be Opal's connection to the outside world.

Although the next few weeks were a challenge, Annie was determined to get Opal to accept her. She kept showing up, bringing drinking water and canned items from her own root cellar. Even though it was winter, Annie noticed that Opal's garden fed the goats and deer more than it did Opal. And, Opal gradually realized she needed someone other than Willy to talk to; now that Della was gone Opal had no one to confide in.

Once Annie felt comfortable, she brought her daughters to visit Aunt Opal. Maggie and Terry found Opal and Willy fascinating. Willy carried them around on his shoulders with Opal and Annie following closely behind ready to catch them if they fell. Annie knew instinctively that Opal needed this contact with the outside world, and she was pleasantly surprised when Opal took to them. It was a strange relationship but it seemed to take an edge off Opal. Annie didn't know Opal's full history and Opal didn't offer to tell her. But Annie did hear bits and pieces from Willy when he was around during her early visits, and others from some of the family.

Annie's persistance paid off. One day—out of the blue—Opal called Annie and invited her over. Thus began the close relationship with Annie and the girls. Opal came to rely more and more on this new family. Annie brought water and food to provide good nutrition, to compensate for bad habits Opal had picked up from Willy. Annie slowly helped Opal thaw her solitude from the world; she still wouldn't leave the property but Annie knew she was succeeding when she would get Opal to laugh.

The one-room school down the road closed, and school busses started coming up on the Ridge to ferry students to the schools in Beaver Creek. In late spring and early fall, the nieces would often get off the bus at Opal's lane and walk down to her cabin to visit. Annie would pick them up, or they would walk the two miles home. Often, Opal had fresh baked cookies for them, and fresh goat milk, at which they usually turned their noses up. As children can do, they overlooked the deficiencies in Opal's character; although they occasionally made fun of her behind her back. In front of Opal, Maggie and Terry were supportive and kind.

Nine

MAY OF 1958 BEGAN with three days of rain. April had been dry, with no rain for two weeks; the spring greening had halted and grasses headed out. Now, the cactus bloomed. Opal loved the claret cup cactus with its fiery red blossoms—never picking them since they weren't like normal flowers with stems and leaves. She wandered the property on this spring day, finding claret cups where she'd never noticed them before.

Willy wasn't feeling well, so he stayed indoors all day. This usually bothered Opal since he always got under her skin when he did this. He wasn't a big reader, but on May 3, he absent-mindedly thumbed through the last year's accumulation of *Look* magazines. He laughed at the cartoons and cursed an article on Vice President Nixon. Willy was a life-long Roosevelt Democrat, starting with Teddy (a Republican, but not one of those 'do-nothings that caused the Depression'), and continuing with FDR.

"You done with this issue?" Willy asked Opal as she threw another chunk of wood into the cookstove. She was making cornbread, one of Willy's favorites.

"Just waitin' to throw it away. I read them when I get them, Willy. I'm not like you and wait six months to glance at it. World out there is changing fast and I need to keep up on it."

"Hell, woman," Willy chuckled and coughed, "you don't even know what's out there in that world. You haven't left this place in years."

"No need to when I can just read about it," Opal laughed. "Why go out. Got what I need here."

"Yeah, you count on me bringing it to you. What you do if I weren't here?" Willy coughed again, a condition that was getting worse, thought Opal.

"Sometimes, Willy, you aren't here. You been moving in slow motion all spring." She put the pan of cornbread in the stove. Smoke came out when she opened the fire door to check the flames. Willy coughed more.

"Rheumatism's eating my bones. My knees been hurtin' something terrible." Willy didn't tell her that when he went down to the creek the day before, he fell three times on the way back up. It took him ten minutes to reach the top—he used to make it in about two.

"Then go lay down and take a nap," Opal snapped at him. She had things to do and he was starting to get on her nerves. She had gotten used to Willy, warts and all, but sometimes she wondered what it would be like to live without him. Their relationship could be likened to an uneasy truce between warring enemies. They needed each other in ways they didn't realize. Opal was accustomed to the 'amenities' Willy brought onto the property and didn't even worry anymore about his 'thieving' as she called it.

The next day, the rain storms moved east and the robins and blue-birds were singing and twittering. Willy got up early since he couldn't sleep. He stood in the open porch door looking south. There was a light touch of snow on the very top of Sheep Mountain. The dry spring had melted the light winter snowpack almost all the way to the top of the mountain. Only the highest nearby peaks still had snow. He thought about the lack of irrigation water this would mean.

Willy walked outside and relieved himself. He zipped his pants as he wandered over to the depleted woodpile. He didn't relish the thought of acquiring and cutting another year's supply of firewood. Leaning over to pick up a few pieces of wood so Opal could have enough for breakfast, he felt a sharp pain in his chest. It radiated up his shoulder and down his arm. He gasped for breath as the pain nearly doubled him over. He saw a flash of light as he looked down. Another stab of pain knocked him to the ground. He yelled for Opal as he rolled over. His eyes closed. They never opened again.

Opal was still in bed when she thought she heard Willy call her. She mumbled something, then turned over. A few minutes later the sun broke through the few remaining clouds on the eastern horizon, and rays of light hit her in the face. She had forgotten to close the curtains the night before.

After a minute, she raised up out of bed and noticed Willy was not in his bed on the porch. He usually got up before her so she wasn't sur-prised. "Willy, you old goat, you might as well live outside with the rest of the goats. You spend more time out there than in here. I guess that is good, though." She got no response to that.

Throwing off the covers and pulling on an old shirt and pair of pants, she looked around the cabin but didn't see Willy. "Hey old man, I thought you'd have the stove going. Cold this morning." Still no response.

"Willy, what use are you when I have to do everything around here? Bring in some wood."

Opal put on her wool socks and pulled on her boots. She wrapped herself with a shawl and grabbed the wood bucket. She opened the door and stood in the sun. Steam rose from the wet ground. She looked around, screamed, dropped the bucket and ran to Willy, sprawled lifeless on the ground. She reached down to pull him up, hoping he had fallen down and was slow to get up. His arm flopped as she let it go.

"Oh God no, Willy. Damn you all to hellfire! Willy!" She shook him, but she knew he would never again move. She looked around again. "I got to get help. Willy, I'll help. Hold on." Opal rubbed her eyes, still not totally free from sleep. She knew instinctively that Willy was dead. Now what was she going to do? Go get help. She would go to the neighbors'. What else could she do? She cursed Willy regularly, but now the reality hit her like a club. Willy was not there anymore.

After shutting the dogs in the cabin, Opal started walking up the lane. Talking to herself helped build her courage. "Willy was right. I never leave the place anymore. I haven't visited anyone but family for years. What have I become?" She quickened her pace. She would go to the Cooper's. They were the closest neighbor. She had never even met them and wasn't sure what their first names were. "Alice," she thought. "Maybe Frank. Or Ben. Yes, Alice, I'm sure of."

She noticed the horses in Cooper's pasture. A few lambs were frolicking in the last field—old man Hertzman's place. She thought maybe he had painted the house red since she last paid attention to it. Maybe not. Willy usually got the mail. All they ever got was his pension check and the cream check. A few catalogs. The Sears catalog was good, she thought. She let him take care of all that.

As she reached the road, she looked both ways for traffic. Few cars ever drove by, but Opal didn't know that. She rarely came out here. She would have to now. "Willy isn't here anymore to do all this. What will I do? Damn," she thought. "I let Willy do most of the things I should have been doing. How did I let this happen? I came here all those years ago to be on my own. Now I'll be on my own again and I've gotten used to him taking care of me. Maybe not taking care, but at least helping."

She was her own person. Had been since she came back from California. "How long ago was that? My God, it was over 20 years ago—maybe 30?" Life didn't change much down at the cabin. The view didn't change. The birds were the same. Same rocks, same trees. What had she allowed to happen?

Opal was stumbling as she walked up to the front door of the white house; she didn't notice the yellow and red tulips blooming in the beds on both sides of the steps. She pounded with her fist, holding back tears. She hadn't cried in years. She wouldn't let anyone see her cry. Alice Cooper opened the door and said, "Why, it's Opal, isn't it? Something is wrong. What is the matter? Frank! Come here, it's Opal."

"Willy is dead. I need help. Willy is dead. He's on the ground. I don't..." Opal stopped as she stared at Alice.

"Frank, call the sheriff. Quick, get a doctor out here. It's Willy Long." Alice held out her hand to Opal, who quickly backed off.

"Oh you poor dear, come in. We're getting help."

Opal backed off the steps, shifting her shawl around her. "No, I have to get back. You will help me?" She looked back south towards her place. Strange, she thought, she had never been here before. These were her neighbors and she had never met them. Alice seemed like a nice lady, about her own age. "I have to get back. Please send someone." She turned and started walking back to the road.

Alice ran out after her. "Opal, please wait. Frank is calling now. Someone will be here. Please let us take you back."

Opal didn't even turn around to look at her. She was walking aimlessly back towards her cabin. Opal didn't hear any more of what Alice was saying. By that time, Frank was out the door, heading for his truck.

"Come on Alice, let's at least follow her. If she doesn't want to ride, that's up to her. She is crazy anyway. Sheriff is on his way. Will take a while to get up here. Let's go down and do what we can."

"She just walked off, Frank. I don't think she even wants us." Alice went in to get her jacket, then got in the truck with Frank who had pulled up in front of the door.

"Alice, do you realize how much courage it took for that woman to walk up here? That old hermit lady screwed up every ounce of courage she ever owned to walk up and knock on our door. My God, if Willy is dead, what will she do? She hasn't done anything by herself since before we moved here."

"That's at least five years," Alice mumbled. "How do you help someone who doesn't want any help at all."

"She is our neighbor. We will do what we can."

Opal was halfway down her lane by the time Frank caught up to her. Frank drove up next to her and stopped. Opal stopped and touched the truck. "Opal, the sheriff is on his way. Would you like to ride the rest of the way?"

Opal shook her head no. "I need to get back to Willy." She started walking faster.

Frank sat there while Opal kept walking. "Damnedest thing, Alice. She looks like a ghost. Remember when your dad died. Your mom had a similar look. Death does something strange to you. Different people deal with it in different ways. Wonder what happened to Willy. Last time I saw him, he looked a little puffy in the face."

"He always looked kind of puffy to me," Alice said as she shook her head. "Poor old lady. I wonder how old she is. I had the feeling she was our age, but she looks terrible."

"How would you look if you found me dead?"

"Oh, Frank, what a terrible thing to say," Alice said as she punched his shoulder.

Frank drove slowly, staying behind Opal as she hurried on ahead. They got to the cabin where Frank stopped and they both got out. This was the first time Alice had been here, but Frank had been down several times to talk to Willy; once was when their horse had gotten through the fence and Frank had to go look for it. Willy laughed about it and Frank was convinced Willy would have kept the horse and never said a word if he hadn't gone looking for it.

Alice saw the body before Frank. "There he is, Frank. Sprawled out right where he fell. Looks dead as a log, doesn't he?"

"Nice sympathy you have there. They may both be strange but let's show a little dignity."

Ignoring the dogs barking in the cabin, Opal stooped over Willy's body. The face and hands were slightly blue, Alice noticed. She also noticed that there were still no tears in Opal's eyes.

Frank pulled Opal up and motioned for Alice to take her inside. "Opal, there is nothing you can do here. The sheriff is on his way. They will take Willy. You need to take care of yourself now." Frank didn't want to deal with Opal, but who else was there? He thought she had relatives, but who were they?

Alice led Opal into the cabin, wincing as she walked in. The two dogs and three cats scurried out when they opened the door, and the dogs hightailed it down to the creek. Alice looked around as she entered; it was dirty, although she could tell they had made some effort to make it homey. As she used to joke, you could tell someone lived in a place and didn't just have it for show. A lived-in house, well, just looked lived in, and not like those houses in the slick magazines. In this cabin, newspapers were serving as wallpaper, held on by canning lids nailed on. Alice smiled at the full-page newspaper advertisement 'Vote for Eisenhower and Nixon.'

Opal hurried over and shut the door to an extra room. She obviously didn't like having someone in her house. She motioned for Alice to sit down on a kitchen chair. Alice brushed it off and reluctantly sat. "Would you like some coffee?" Alice asked, noticing a coffee pot on the stove.

"Stove ain't lit. Willy usually did that for me."

"Would you like me to start a fire?" Alice really didn't want to. She was appalled by the stack of newspapers and kindling laying right up against the stove. Empty cans were piled on the floor along the wall.

"No, I'm fine." Opal stared at the stove.

Frank walked in. "Opal, is there a blanket I can use to cover him? I don't like him just lying there."

Opal looked at the back room. She didn't want these strangers in her bedroom. "Here, take my shawl." She started to take it off.

"You keep that Opal. I may have a blanket in the truck." Frank walked out the door and rummaged behind the seat. There were empty grain bags. He didn't like the idea of using those. He started to take off his jacket when he saw the sheriff's car coming down the lane. He got here sooner than Frank expected. "Thank goodness," Frank mouthed to himself. He stood and waited.

Sheriff Wilson stopped behind Frank's pickup, got out and walked over to the body.

"Mornin' sheriff. Looks like old Willy just fell over dead. Opal is inside." The sheriff said nothing but nodded to Frank. He leaned over and put his head next to Willy's face. He calmly walked back to his car and got back in. Frank heard him talking on his radio but didn't listen. He stared off to the south. He realized the view from the cabin was a view worthy of many mansions. The mountains were crisp and clear with their fresh coating of snow on the very tops. He liked the view from their house, but this was completely different, and not even a half-mile away and slightly downhill. The ground fell off sharply beyond the cabin and to the sides.

Sheriff Wilson pulled out a pad of paper, then pulled a can of tobacco from his shirt pocket and stuffed a wad in his mouth. "Coroner is coming up with the ambulance. He needs to declare the death. They will take Willy to the morgue. We will have to talk to Opal about arrangements. Think she can handle it? She seems a bit crazy to me. The few times I've encountered her was when she was threatening folks with her shotgun. I need to talk to her about details, but you give me what you know first."

Frank asked, "Do you have someone from the county who can come up and look after her? Social people or something like that? We can help but that woman is really strange and we don't feel comfortable. She ain't like normal people. You got that right."

Opal knew the sheriff was outside, but she didn't want to go out. What were they doing out there? She was very uncomfortable with Alice just sitting at her table. Alice tried small talk, but Opal didn't care about what she was talking about. No one else knew what Opal was going through. All these strangers on her property, sitting in her kitchen, looking into her private life.

Ten

EVER SINCE SHE HAD assumed Willy's last name, Opal was known in the community as Opal Long, Willy's wife. After she assumed his last name, she had used it so long, sometimes she forgot who she really was. Willy would do that to you. He had stolen so many things from people, he also stole Opal's identity.

Well—now that would have to change. Opal looked out the window as the ambulance silently drove up. Two doors slammed as two men got out and removed a wheeled stretcher. She didn't want to, but was drawn to watch. The body disappeared under a sheet, then it was wheeled into the ambulance. The sheriff pointed and all four of the men looked towards the cabin. She couldn't hear what they were saying, but she knew they were talking about her. A lot of people would talk about her now. She frowned. It was nobody's business.

"Nobody's damn business," Opal said out loud.

Alice had been watching Opal intently, trying to figure out how she would react. Now she perked up. "I'm sorry, what did you say?" She looked out the window. Frank was walking over to the cabin.

"You people are trespassing. It's nobody's business what happens to me. I've done fine up here for years. I keep to myself and I don't bother you. I don't want nobody's sympathy. I just want to be left alone."

Frank entered the cabin and put his hand on Alice's shoulder. "Come on Alice, it's time to go." He walked up to Opal and handed her Willy's pocket watch. "This was all he had on him. Opal, we will leave you now. We will honor your wishes, but you did come to us for help. We are your neighbors and if you need anything, we would like to help in any way we can. I want to get along with all my neighbors." Regardless of how stubborn and obstinate they are—he thought to himself. He looked into Opal's eyes for a few seconds, to try and reach through the wall she had erected.

"Thank you," Opal said as she looked down at the watch. She swung it back and forth on its long chain. "You are good people."

Frank wanted to put his arm around her, but he knew better. He started to walk out the door, following Alice. "The sheriff will come over here in a minute. He needs to do some paperwork. He will tell you what they will do with the body. With Willy." He had to be kind. It might be a body, but it was Willy. Opal knew him as Willy, not a body.

Opal started to say something but stopped. She let Frank and Alice walk out the door. They talked to the sheriff for several minutes, then got in their truck and drove off. The ambulance had already driven off. Opal didn't want anyone else in her cabin, so she walked out to meet the sheriff who was starting to walk towards her.

"Opal, I need you to write just a couple sentences on what you saw. When you saw Willy and what you saw or heard. Then sign it. Is that all right with you? That's all I need. A few more things, then I will leave you alone. Someone from the funeral home will telephone you. I will tell them to come up here unless you want me to take you into town. Willy will be there. If you want a service, they will help. We will need to notify any other close relatives. Do you need help with that?"

Opal scribbled a sentence on the top sheet of the paper pad the sheriff handed her, then signed her name. She looked up at him and said softly, "No one else cares. Willy had two sons but they never talked. Hadn't seen 'em for years. I'm all he had. We can't afford nothin'. Might as well bring him back up here and plant him. Can't pay for no funeral." She shook her head as she handed him the witness statement.

The sheriff smiled to himself as he read: 'I walked out and saw Willy laying dead on the ground. Opal Long.' "Don't worry, Opal, the county can take care of it. Everyone deserves a proper burial. It will be in the Beaver Creek cemetery if that's all right with you."

"It's nobody's business," Opal repeated, almost by rote. "I don't want no sympathy or anything like that."

The sheriff was surprised at himself. He was being very calm and compassionate with this stubborn old hermit. As he looked at her, he realized she probably wasn't that old. He wanted to drive off and forget about her, but he knew he might have to get someone from the County social services to come out, and he would also contact a church in town. Heaven help them when they drove up with food or whatever they did. It would test their compassion, but they were trained for that. Maybe she would react better. He was often surprised at the immediate reaction of people when a loved one died. It was hard to tell what they would say at the time, only to act like a totally different person later.

As far as Opal was concerned, it was over and done with. Time to move on. She had walked away from her life when she left to go to California. Then she walked away from California to start over again here. When she left Thad and Della's house to come live up here, she walked away once more, for good. She couldn't walk away from here, but she would close the book on Willy and start over once again. She didn't want people coming onto her property and she certainly didn't need do-gooders feeling sorry for her.

In the afternoon, do-gooders did come. As soon as the two ladies stopped their car, Opal was standing beside the driver's door before they even tried to get out. The driver rolled the window down and Opal told them she didn't need them. Her abruptness shocked the passenger, but the driver introduced herself. "I'm Sarah Jewelson. I don't know you and you don't know us, but we want to offer any help we can. I lost my husband three years ago and at first I felt bitter and didn't want people helping. Then, I realized I did need help. We don't want to intrude, but we want you to know people are willing to help."

Opal felt odd about this. She wasn't used to talking to strangers anymore. She used to be good at talking to people. That is what she did in her job in Oakland years ago. She just wanted to get on with her new life without Willy and these people made her nervous.

"Don't need no help and don't need people feeling sorry for me. You drove up here for nothing." Opal started to turn away, and the driver opened the door and got out. She opened the back door of the car and pulled out a cardboard box. She held it out to Opal, who didn't take it.

"It's just some fried chicken and a cake and a few other things. Our church was having a luncheon today and we thought you might like some." She looked at the box, then at Opal.

"Can't afford that fancy stuff." Opal wanted the ladies to go.

"Oh, it's from us to you. We always make extra. Our gift." When Opal still didn't offer to take it, the woman set the box on the ground and got back in her car. "We are sorry for your loss. Eat this if you want. We just want to be neighborly. If there is anything we can do to help, please let us know. My name and phone number are written on a piece of paper in the box."

She backed the car around, with Opal still standing there. Her passenger said, "My lord, Sarah, I've never seen anyone so ungrateful. She was downright rude."

"Mavis, I've seen all kinds. We heard that she is strange. Now we know. People do act strange when they lose a loved one. Remember me—I was angry, then scared. I may have said things I regretted when I lost Robert. We came up here to help. If she doesn't want help, then that's up to her. Don't take it personal."

~

Two hours later, a black car drove up and before Opal could meet it, a man in a gray suit was walking over to her where she was in her rocking chair on the porch. He noticed a box lying on the ground; it was torn into pieces, with a goat chewing on the remains of a paper plate. Opal rose and came down the steps. "I don't need anything, so you might as well turn around." He smiled and handed her a card. She took it, looked at it briefly, and tried to hand it back to him. He told her to keep it. "I'm Carl Abernathy, from the funeral home. I need to talk to you about Mr. Long."

"I can't afford a funeral. Just bring Willy up here. I'll dig a grave and put him there." Mr. Abernathy suppressed a smile as he told her she couldn't do that. "Mr. Long needs a burial in the cemetery. In cases like this, the county will bury him. Is there a suit coat or nice clothes?" Opal spit out a laugh and said, "Willy rarely took a bath, much less had decent clothes."

Mr. Abernathy asked if Willy had other close relatives. Opal mentioned the sons but didn't know where they lived. "I will write an obituary and would appreciate it if you will tell me what you know about Mr. Long." He was surprised when Opal briefly stared off at the distant mountains, then invited him inside, and then she told him the little she knew about Willy.

Mr. Abernathy was accustomed to working with grieving people. It was his job and he was good at it. He managed to help Opal open up. After fifteen minutes, Opal got up and went to a dresser in the side room. He started to follow her, but she shook her head no and closed the door behind her. The undertaker looked around the cabin, and shook his head as he noticed the various indicators of severe poverty:

bare board floor, newspaper wallpaper, the empty cans and bottles, a few rag rugs, no pictures on the walls, no indications of a home life or attachment to anything of beauty. He could hear Opal opening drawers in the other room. He heard what sounded like a sob, followed by an intake of breath, then what sounded like "damn you old man." He had seen some poor people in this county, but nothing like this cabin.

After a few minutes, Opal came out , closing the door behind her. She handed Mr. Abernathy a white shirt, black slacks, and a worn old brown sport coat. "These belonged to my step-father. Willy didn't have anything nice. No going-to-town clothes you would say. He was a rough man, simple. I'm sure you could make these fit. Guess it doesn't matter if they fit or not. Would be more proper to put on new overalls and plaid shirt, but he didn't have none."

"Are you sure you want to part with these? If they belonged to someone else..."

"No good to me. And old Thad sure don't need them anymore. He died a few years ago. This is Ma's room."

"Oh, I'm sorry, I didn't know anyone else lived here," Mr. Abernathy quickly added.

"She doesn't live here. She lived up the road, but this was her room."

Mr. Abernathy looked at Opal for more of an explanation, but Opal was finished saying all she was going to say. He took the clothes, thinking it was simpler to take them, then get better clothes from one of the churches or charities. This would be a pauper's funeral. He wouldn't put much into a casket or funeral, but the county would pay for it anyway. "I'll plan for the graveside service in three days, and send someone to take you into town. What would you like for services?" She just shook her head. He continued, "Do you have any nice clothes to wear?" He stifled a laugh when Opal said no one would be there except Willy and he sure the hell didn't care what she wore.

She was right about the service. Mr. Abernathy, the Beaver Creek Baptist minister (whom she didn't know), and Opal were the only ones to stand by the simple wood casket. (Annie and Rand and the girls were visiting Annie's cousin in North Park.) The minister said a few very nice words and gave Opal the paper he read from. Mr. Abernathy almost teared up as Opal walked over and laid the paper and a bouquet of flowers tied in string on the casket. This simple lady, pathetic in her loneliness, gave what she had, then walked away. Mr. Abernathy looked at the minister, then down at the wilted irises and faded lilacs. There were so many types of people he dealt with in his line of work. He would remember this one for years; he knew there would never be a headstone, nor a single person who would ever come to pay any respects at this grave. He sighed to himself, "Mrs. Long was right—we probably should have planted him on Bean Ridge, by the log cabin with its fantastic view." He drove Opal back up there, neither of them saying a word.

Eleven

WITH WILLY GONE FOREVER, Opal found herself missing the old coot. She had said to herself so many times that she wouldn't mind if he disappeared and never came back. She made him sleep outside more times than she let him sleep in his bed inside. The land and the cabin were hers and Willy knew that.

Opal was true to her vow and didn't let herself cry over his death. However, something left Opal's life when she walked away from his grave in the Beaver Creek cemetery. Willy had been her companion and nearly her only friend. He knew enough about Opal to understand her behavior; as with many other things, he didn't care. Over the years, Opal had lost parts of her life, never gaining anything new to replace it. She knew she was becoming a hollow shell. Willy had been the structure that held that shell together.

In the following months, Opal planted her garden and mended broken fences. She threw out most of Willy's clothes and used quite a few for rags and chinking between the cabin's logs. Some of the logs were old and rotten—she could see patches of blue sky between the higher logs. Willy had occasionally mixed concrete to fill in gaps, but Opal didn't know how to prepare the mix and he had used the last of the bags he had brought from who-knows-where.

During one of Annie's visits the next year, Opal asked her to go out to the root cellar to get a jar of jam for the bread she had baked that morning. The cellar was next to the cabin, under the apricot tree. Since Willy was not there to make repairs to the rock, earth and log roof, it was starting to sag. Annie usually avoided going into the cellar, but she took a deep breath and ducked under the sagging door frame. She was appalled at the difference from the last time she was down there. Dust was covering the shelves; one side of the cellar was just cartons full of empty jars. She looked for jam but found only one. It looked like strawberry, with a label hand-printed by Opal. Annie picked it up and read: "The last jam I made for Willy. 1957." She held it and thought, "maybe Opal cared more for Willy than she let on. What a sad thought, that Opal would write this on the label after Willy died." She set it back on the shelf and went back to the cabin and told Opal she couldn't find any jam.

~

In the spring of 1959, Opal was sitting on her porch in her rocking chair, listening to Puccini's *Madame Butterfly*. She loved the aria "Un bel di vedremo." She even knew what it meant in English: One fine day we shall see. She had over the years been able to learn the lyrics to many of the songs, but she usually didn't listen to the words. She found *Butterfly* especially moving. She had cried at the opening performance when Alberto took her to the Opera House in San Francisco. As she was re-living the first time she had heard the song, a pickup drove up to the cabin, interrupting her memories.

An older man got out of the Ford and walked over to Opal. He was wearing fancy boots with mud-stained jeans and an expensive-looking wool shirt. He took off his straw Stetson and nodded his head to Opal. She stared at him, surprised at his sudden appearance. Very seldom did anyone drive onto her property. Often, she put the fence gate across the lane, but either she had forgotten that day or the man had opened it and come on in. Either way, she was not pleased to see a stranger standing before her.

"Howdy ma'am," the man said, as he stood holding his hat. "My name is Barrett James. Folks call me Bear." He waited for her to introduce herself but Opal just stared, saying nothing.

"I am sorry to intrude on you like this. Sounds like you are enjoying, what is it, Verdi?"

"Puccini, and who said you could trespass on my place? You came in, so you obviously know the way back out." She looked back on the porch to see if her shotgun was handy. It wasn't. The record had stopped playing by then.

What they had said about her was true, he thought. He wasn't sure how to go about this, so he just blurted out his rehearsed statement. "I apologize. I should have called first. I will leave but before I go, I want to ask a question. I am interested in buying your west 40 acres. I understand you lost your husband a year or two back and I am looking to move to this area. I thought maybe you might like to reduce the amount of land you have to keep up by yourself." He waited for a response but heard only long seconds of silence.

Opal continued to stare at him, saying nothing.

Bear shifted back and forth, not knowing what to do next. This old lady intrigued him: tattered old clothes, with uncombed, dirty hair sticking out from beneath an old felt hat. Despite this, he thought he could detect something hidden under her appearance. He thought to himself, "this woman is very troubled and hiding something. She probably isn't as old as I think."

Finally, Opal stood up and said, "Maybe you didn't hear me. You can back up and turn around at the fence line. Your truck made it in here fine, I'm sure it will head back out just as well."

"It's Mrs. Long, isn't it? I respect your privacy, but I really am interested in buying your west forty. I will give you a very fair price. It is a lot of land for one woman to take care of. I will build a fence on the line so you don't have to do a thing. I will even get an official survey." He stared back at her.

Anyone watching would have laughed at the apparent standoff. Both stood staring at each other. You could almost see the wheels turning in each of their heads. Bear thought he saw a faint smile on Opal's face.

Opal finally looked away. "Mr. Bear, come back tomorrow at this same time. I will think it over." She looked past him to the property stretching to the west. "Why here? You can't make a living on that piece of sagebrush and cedars. And I don't want any neighbors closer than I got."

Bear smiled. "Mrs. Long, I may be just like you. Wanting to get away from people. I've made my living. I just want to watch the sun set every evening. You'll never know I was there. Thank you for considering it. I will see you tomorrow." He turned, put his hat back on his balding head, and got in his truck. He slowly backed up, watching Opal as long as he could. He turned around and drove the long bumpy lane back to the road.

Annie came by later that afternoon, bringing groceries and a large jug of drinking water. Opal told her of the stranger and his offer. Annie raised her eyebrows in surprise.

"Opal, did he say how much? That might be what you need. Some extra cash. You don't use that land anyway. It won't feed a cow. You know that twenty acres north of us? It sold last week for twice what the Mitchells paid for it only three years ago. More people are coming up here and land is worth more. This might be your chance. You let me know what he offers. He will go low. If you hold out for more, he will probably give it. Don't promise anything 'til you talk to Rand and me. Promise?"

Two weeks later, Opal sold the 40 acres for more money than she had ever had in her life. She didn't understand why he wanted it, but she hardly ever set foot on it and the fence on the west side needed a lot of work. As he had promised, he built a new three-wire fence. It wasn't very tight and many of the posts were scraggly juniper branches, but it was a sight better than what existed on the far west boundary. Opal didn't have a bank account and she had Annie help her cash the check and put the money in jars which she put in Della's room. Annie tried to talk her out of that but to no avail.

Opal didn't see much of Bear for the first few months, but she would see his Ford drive onto the sagebrush flat and hear the door slam. At first, he pulled in a beat-up travel trailer, then he built a three-sided shed. He would be there for a week or two at a time, then he would disappear for weeks. One day, he walked over to her cabin, surprising her as she walked out of the outhouse.

"Morning, Opal, fine day isn't it?"

"I told you once and I won't tell you again. I don't want to ever see you on this place. I sold you enough land for you to disappear on. Go disappear."

Bear smiled. "Yes, indeed, it is a fine day. Look at that blue sky. Opal, I want to build a small cabin right along the fence line."

"I told you I don't want to see you or a small cabin, but you do what you want on your own property."

"Well, one small problem with that thought. I picked out just what I think is a perfect spot and it happens to be about five feet onto your property." Bear pulled a stick of gum out of his pocket and offered it to Opal. She ignored him.

She stared at him a full thirty seconds before she spoke. Bear slowly unwrapped the gum and put it in his mouth.

"Old man, are you crazy? You sittin' in the sun for too long? Do you think I am crazy? I sell you 40 acres, enough to hide a herd of elephants on and you want to build your house on my land?" Opal laughed, something Bear had not experienced before.

"I will pay you for it. It's only a few feet across the line. It is nice and flat and has a better view than further back on my place." Bear had rehearsed his reasons, but they weren't coming out very well. He realized now how stupid it sounded. "It's on your land. It will belong to you. I will live in it while I am here."

"While you are here? Where else do you plan to live?"

"Oh I will live here, but I travel a lot. I don't want a big place, just a two-room cabin, with a kitchen-living room, and a bedroom next to it. Nothing fancy."

"Well go build your nothing-fancy place on your own property." Opal was tired of talking with him. She turned and started to walk away.

"I will pay you $1000 for the right to build it."

"I am walking into the house to get my shotgun. When I walk back out, I will count to five before I shoot your toes off. Then I will aim higher, for that empty head of yours that doesn't have a brain in it." Opal walked into the cabin.

Bear knew she was crazy enough to do it. He had heard stories of her running off neighbors with that shotgun. He turned and muttered "damned old lady. She is the crazy one." As he approached the fence and was about to climb over, he heard a shotgun blast. He turned and saw Opal holding the gun pointed up in the air. She was laughing as she turned to walk back into her cabin. "Holy Harry. That woman is going to kill someone yet."

Bear did build his cabin on his property, right up against the fence. Several years later, the next owner of Bear's 40 acres had the property line re-surveyed: the fence was offline by 15 feet. When the fence was rebuilt by the new owner, the cabin sat on the very edge of Opal's property. She often thought of tearing it down or burning it, but by then, it was too much trouble. Except for two times she rented it to a friend of Willy's, it sat vacant. Even that gesture of having someone living nearby was a difficult one that Opal fussed over before saying yes. She needed some money—evidently she had forgotten about the money in jars in Ma's room from the sale of the property.

~

After Annie and Rand's third daughter, Betsy, was born, Annie spent more time visiting Opal. Opal was delighted with the new baby and actually enjoyed the visits. All the girls got a kick out of their crazy aunt, but as the years went by, they visited less often. Their friends on the mesa were scared of the old Goat Lady, so were cautious about keeping company with Opal's nieces. They said their parents warned them not to go down to that old cabin and the crazy woman with the shotgun. Annie tried to convince them Opal was harmless, but there were too many stories and rumors circulating; her appearance deteriorated further, and she was scary to look at, in her old-man clothes, floppy hat, and dirty appearance.

As Terry, Maggie and Betsy reached their teens, they spent more time with classmates in town. She had gotten used to their visits, needed them more than she realized, and didn't want to lose their company. She couldn't relate to teenage girls any more than she could relate to anyone else. If her goat milk and cookies wouldn't keep them coming, she had to find something that would. Opal did not feel comfortable talking to anyone else, but she enjoyed the excitement her nieces had for life. So she started telling them stories, partly of her own life in California, and partly made up or greatly enhanced. She left out the ugly parts of her marriage and late husband, and only told the humorous parts of the Willy part of her life; he had too much of a borrowing-appropriating reputation, so she emphasized the sillier things he did—like digging a hole so deep for one of their cisterns, he couldn't get out and had to spend a cold damp night in the mud. Or when he tangled with the old billy goat, the goat winning of course, and Willy having to go to the hospital and get 20 stitches in his groin.

Deer were increasing each year, and some winters a herd of 50 to 100 elk would bed down on the east ridge. Willy would have shot several for their supply of meat, but Opal didn't like to butcher them, and besides, her aim with the rifle was so poor she probably couldn't kill one if it were standing next to her. Every year, she realized more and more how much she had depended on Willy.

The year after Willy died—while rummaging in a shed for something else—Opal discovered a half-dozen rolls of 'new' wallpaper that

Willy had given her years ago and forgotten. Since the rolls were barely chewed by mice or rats, and the flower pattern was colorful, Opal decided to use it in the cabin. She was tired of some of the news in the newspaper-wallpaper, so on one wall she tacked up the flowery paper over the newspapers with more canning jar lids and nails. That way, she could still read old news and advertisements as she ate or sat by the fire on a cold night, and, have flowers, too. Annie was appalled when she saw what Opal had done, but Rand just shrugged when she told him about it. His only comment was "what more can we expect from the old woman? God, Annie, how many times do we have this discussion? She is beyond help. Just let her live in her little world. She is not hurting anyone." He comforted Annie the best he could as she cried herself to sleep on many nights after her visits with Opal.

The lilacs she and Willy planted had thrived and filled the area between the cabin and garden with sweet-smelling purple in May or late April, along with white spirea and honeysuckle. Moths and bees and flies and butterflies covered the blooms. The silver poplar trees grew larger, and the irises spread by themselves over the years. The roses spread up against the cabin and added brilliant yellows in June. And in mid-summer, the Bouncing Bets filled the area with large pale pink and white blossoms. Although Opal lived a simple life, uncluttered by what most people considered the attractive comforts of a normal home, she did have a colorful yard. There was no lawn since she had no watering system, but there was enough tailwater from the fields above her to keep the flowers and bushes and trees alive and almost healthy.

Within the few hundred yards that comprised Opal's world, other things changed after Willy's passing. She no longer had a milk cow. Old Gertie lay as a pile of hide and bones down at the bottom of the draw which now carried more water. Coyotes and mountain lions had scattered the bones quickly as the old cow mired down in the mud one wet winter and was too old and tired to break free of the knee-deep bog. Several goats occasionally wandered the property, more often than not going through the fence to Mr. Bollard's fields to the east; he finally rebuilt the fence along his property line, forcing the goats to wander into the fields north of Opal. Half-starved if they stayed on Opal's place, they eventually fell victim one by one to the same coyotes and lions. Now Opal had only her cats and dogs. Most of the chickens had lost their struggle against the foxes and coyotes years ago.

Determined to have laying hens so she could eat fresh eggs, Opal patched and patched the fence around her chicken coop. She stole rusted wire from her other fences to repair the hen house, but the chicks that Annie bought from the feed store never lasted long enough to lay a single egg. Opal cursed all wild four-leggeds, not realizing her own dogs and cats were the guilty parties half of the time.

Opal struggled to tend the vegetable garden north of the cabin. Willy had been able to keep the fence up and effective, but without him to mend it, her attempts failed. She had it so tangled with chicken wire, barbed wire, baling wire and boards, that Annie had Rand come on a Sunday afternoon to pull it down. Rand wanted to tear down all the fences on the property, but he knew it would take weeks of very hard labor. Opal told him not to touch the fences since she needed them to keep the cows and goats in. Rand refrained from pointing out that she no longer had cows and goats.

Twelve

Opal was slowing down by 1965 and becoming even more reclusive. The population of the mesa still consisted mostly of hardscrabble ranchers, but a few newcomers were starting to frequent the area. The wiser old-timers realized the gold mine they were sitting on: they couldn't make a living raising cows and pigs, working in the orchards, or other part-time jobs, but they could sell their few acres to these long-haired kids. The long-time residents certainly knew about booze; some of them had supplemented their incomes decades earlier by hiding stills in their juniper patches and selling moonshine to Denver dealers. But few of the locals knew anything about marijuana—an import that came along with the tepees and shacks in the communes springing up on the mesa.

The lifestyle of these newcomers required space and solitude, which fit in well with the attitudes of the old-timers. Each left the other alone, although loud music coming from portable radios and the guitars and drums bothered many locals. Opal's nearest neighbors were used to hearing music as Opal played her increasingly scratchy Puccini records during good weather; the old-timers considered opera a far sight better than the Rolling Stones and other so-called music.

Opal was sitting on her porch one warm May afternoon, slowly rocking back and forth in her rickety chair, when an old battered Jeep drove up to the cabin. As was her habit, her first response was to pick up her shotgun. The Jeep honked, then the driver waited a few seconds before he opened the door and got out. He had heard that the polite way to visit Native Americans was to do this. This Easterner had no idea if the owner was Indian or not, but he would play by these Western rules. He smiled a toothy grin as he watched Opal walk towards him waving her shotgun.

"You go out the same way you come in." She raised the gun and pointed it at the lanky man in jeans and sandals. His long hair was tied in a ponytail, something that bothered Opal.

"Howdy, ma'am. You are Opal aren't you?" he said as he edged back towards the Jeep door. By this time he was wishing he had taken the advice he'd been given about staying away from the old cabin south of the road. He should at least have brought someone along with him.

"Who I am don't concern you. Who you are don't matter to me, other than you will be full of buckshot if you don't turn around and hightail it off this place. Maybe I will call you Bucky."

"Could I give you something? I am a neighbor. Live down the road about a mile. I brought some fudge my old lady made this morning. It has..." he broke off quickly as he watched Opal raise the gun in the air and pull the trigger—and a shotgun blast roared.

Opal laughed as she lowered the barrel. "I done told you. Leave right now or this next one is aimed for your tires." Her laugh echoed in the juniper branches along with the fading sound of the 16-gauge. She stared at the Jeep, and slowly turned her gaze to the person fumbling with its door handle. She knew that people thought she lacked social skills. She didn't care. She had the skills that helped her survive all these years—those skills simply did not include dealing with any other person.

"Jesus, she's crazy. Just like they said," the young man mumbled. He quickly slid into the driver's seat. He shouted out the window, "my name is Tim. I want to rent a piece of your property. I will come back later. Nice meeting you." He slammed into reverse and sped backward. Luckily he was quicker than Opal as her next shot fell short.

After consulting with friends, Tim wisely decided not to come back. What Opal had missed was an opportunity to rent her east ridge to a half-dozen college dropouts who wanted a place to put up large teepees. They had secretly trespassed and discovered she had water in the draw which they could pump up to their tents as well as water their 'gardens' down in the draw. The location was perfect for their new business. Since Opal no longer walked down to the bottom of her property, she didn't know that Tim continued to trespass. If she had walked to the bottom, she would have had no idea what the black pipe was for; nor would she have recognized the dozens of plants hidden among the cattails and sumac. Tim tended his garden for a couple of years, getting a high price for his Crazy Lady Special weed. When he was busted and disappeared, his friends quietly pulled the pipe and went to the other end of the mesa until they were jailed a year after that. Opal never understood why black helicopters spent so much time flying over her place in early autumn, and the Feds had no idea she occasionally pointed her shotgun in anger at them.

She also didn't know that the mesa was home to several communes of these strange young people. As the newcomers grew older they abandoned the freewheeling lifestyle: one became a real estate broker; a couple became respectable home builders; and others became artisans—crafting jewelry, and juniper and wrought-iron furniture, sold in the expanding ski towns of Vail and Telluride. The mesa was changing, but this meant nothing to Opal since she rarely left her property.

As the hippies faded into history, the respectable business-people who remained changed the mesa. They persuaded the County to start paving roads. Phone and electric lines were improved. Old houses and log cabins were torn down or burned. New ranch-style houses started springing up. More expensive cars and trucks were part of the increasing traffic. School buses now were common since the last one-room schoolhouse had been turned into a community center, and all students now went to school in Beaver Creek.

The last of the orchards was bulldozed. Planted over a half-century earlier, the apple trees struggled to hang on, rarely producing a profitable crop. By the time the last apple tree was cut into firewood, the irrigation water company finished enlarging Spruce Flat Reservoir and lining miles of ditches that tripled the available irrigation water reaching Bean Ridge. More sprinkler systems watered previously sagebrush-filled acres. Pickup-drawn trailers filled with gated pipe zipped past the weedy entrance to Opal's lane. Sitting in her old rocking chair, Opal had no idea the world was changing beyond her patched-together fences.

~

Opal watched one day as a cabin was moved onto the property next door. This was the land once owned by Bear, which sat vacant for years. After the squabble about the cabin, Bear disappeared. She never saw him or anyone else on that land; her curiosity stopped at her fence line and his disappearance gave her no concern.

Now she noticed that a new owner added onto the cabin until it resembled a respectable-looking two-story home. This new neighbor had heard enough about Opal to plan a strategy to meet her. She went to the fence every day and hollered "good morning" to Opal. She even brought a lawn chair, set it next to the fence, and relaxed with an umbrella to read a book. Finally, she cracked the shell of curiosity: Opal walked over to her one morning.

"Good morning Opal," Betty said to a befuddled Opal. "I'm Betty and I know you like your privacy. I do, too. That's why Greg and I moved here. We plan to leave you alone, but I didn't want to intrude on you by walking over to your cabin to meet you."

Opal didn't know what to say. She had never met most of her other neighbors, but this one had a house close enough that she could see them working in their yard. She didn't like that, but she figured maybe these new people might be all right because they didn't come onto her property. "Morning," she said hesitantly, still uncertain of the situation.

"Opal, I do have one favor to ask you. We need to run electricity to our house and we have to run it off the line that runs across your place. We talked to the power company and they said I would have to get an easement from you." Betty didn't tell Opal that the company refused to go onto Opal's place to ask her; or that they relied on Annie to read the meter during her visits, because the last time their meter reader had gone onto the property to read it, Opal ran him off with her shotgun. The linemen wanted to just shut off the power, but the president of the company said he would let her have power free before he would shut her off. He had grown up a few miles down the road and knew about Opal and her eccentricities. She didn't use much power and she was old.

Betty had the easement drawn up and one day during her vigil in the lawn chair, she got Opal to come over and sign it. She gave Opal a hundred-dollar bill to compensate her, and shared a batch of cookies to distract her during a fence line chat, while the power company drove onto the property, and strung the new lines to the new power pole just over the fence line. Betty and Greg now had power and Opal never knew what had happened, and, never noticed the new wires overhead going from her power pole to the new pole.

Opal was starting to get confused about other things. Some mornings she would holler at Willy to start the woodstove, then remember Willy was no longer there, nor had been for years. Occasionally, while she was sitting in the sun listening to one of her records, she asked Alberto when they could go to the next opera.

Even before Willy died, Opal talked to herself much of the time. Now, she enjoyed Annie's visits which gave her a real person to talk to. She especially enjoyed her nieces' visits, but they became infrequent over the years. She received invitations to their weddings, but since she rarely went out to the road to get her mail, she got them too late to attend. She wouldn't have anyway, and the girls all knew that. At Christmas, which Opal did not observe, the nieces would call but she never understood why.

She continued to rely on Annie to bring her large milk cans of drinking water, along with groceries. Willy had been able to fix the pump after it was knocked into the pond by the goats all those years ago, but Opal hadn't tried to repair the system when one day nothing happened as she flipped the switch to turn on the pump.

The trespassing 'gardeners' had altered the pond when they used it to water their pot gardens further down the creek; their black plastic pipes stuck out of the rock dam, which now held mostly mud, cattails, and watercress rather than open water. And the concrete-lined cisterns Opal and Willy painstakingly dug by hand years ago didn't hold water any longer. The tailwater still came down the ditch from the Cooper's field uphill, but there was no way to store it. The huge silver poplar trees, that for years had absorbed this life-giving water, struggled to survive.

Television was a surprise gift to her from Annie and Rand. About the time the pot growers ended their tenure on Opal's property, Rand attached an antenna to the juniper outside her bedroom and ran the wire through the logs. At first, she refused to turn 'that contraption' on, but soon she was hooked on the daily soap operas. She cursed them, mocking the twisted plots, but found herself drawn to *A Guiding Light* and *As the World Turns*. The evening news and commercials brought the outside world to her. She now could converse with Annie and her nieces about pantyhose, breath mints, and underarm deodorant. She laughed at *Beverly Hillbillies* and *Green Acres*, thinking this was the way most people lived. She liked *Gunsmoke* and *Rawhide*, comparing them to the world she grew up in.

She didn't understand about Watergate and thought those evil people were wrongly persecuting Dick Nixon. She told Annie she hadn't voted in many years (possibly never, she had a feeling she did one time), but still had a full-page newspaper ad urging voters to vote for Ike and Dick back in '52 as part of the wallpaper in her kitchen. She asked Annie about getting real curtains for the west windows—because the sunlight disturbed her TV watching.

Opal was confused easily, especially about time. She wondered why she was living so long, not fully understanding that she was not that old. Days turned into years as the outside world continued to change and modernize, a world Opal wouldn't recognize. She continued to survive in her own private place on Bean Ridge.

Opal would sit outside in her rocking chair, playing her Puccini records. As the years went by, she played the music louder since her hearing was going. Frank and the other neighbors knew Opal was sitting and rocking when they heard *Turandot* or *Madam Butterfly* echoing over the alfalfa fields. Frank Cooper had no idea what the music was, but Mr. Henderson told him one night that he recognized some of the music as Puccini operas. Frank referred to her from that point on as the Hermit of Puccini Ridge.

Thirteen

THE ONLY WAY OPAL could keep track of days was by turning on the television. If Dan Rather was on the evening news, it was somewhere between Monday and Friday. That was close enough for her. All that mattered to her was whether it was summer or winter. She hated winter since she could not keep the stove going overnight and it was freezing cold when she woke up in the morning. Although many nice days allowed her to wander around on the main ridge, many cold ones kept her inside. Besides, she was not able to go down the hill to the creek or to walk over to the sage flat. Her knees hurt and she seemed to be out of breath a lot. Age was catching up to Opal. And so was the disease that Paul gave her all those decades ago—his evil still haunting her.

Many mornings, summer or winter, she didn't want to get out of bed at all. The dogs usually took care of that as they pounced on her bed, wrestling with each other, forcing her up to feed them. In the summer, they would push open the screen door and then come back in through a flap of loose screen. Of course, chipmunks came in as well, but the cats would raise a ruckus as they flew in all directions chasing the poor chipmunks; how there could be any chipmunks still alive with the dogs and all the cats was a lesson about the fecundity of the flip-tails. Opal still enjoyed watching them, but didn't recognize the cause-and-effect of her dogs and cats and the havoc they played on birds, squirrels, deer— all the wildlife she used to love.

One day—it must have been a Sunday since her nieces visited on Sundays—she dropped one of her Puccini records and it shattered on the floor when it landed on a rock. What the rock was doing on the floor she didn't know, but she slowly picked up seven pieces of black vinyl and held them in her hand. She had embraced its memories for over 50 years. It was *Turandot*. She would never hear "Nessun Dorma" again—it represented San Francisco and Alberto. She tried to remember Alberto but could no longer see his face or hear his voice. She remembered he was the one good thing that had happened to her in her long life and she had held onto his memory for so long. Now, as she fingered the sharp-edged black pieces, she knew it was time to let him go.

When Terry arrived and saw the broken record, she told Opal she would get her a CD of the opera. "I'll buy a CD player for you, too, and you'll enjoy that more than the old record, because the quality of the recording is so much better." Terry didn't understand why Opal enjoyed the old 78, with its scratches and poor quality.

Even if Terry had asked, Opal would not have been able to articulate that the record was not just the music, but that it transported her back into Alberto's arms; that Alberto himself had bought that actual record and handed it to her, wrapped in shiny red paper with a big lacy bow. She sometimes remembered a photo taken by a street photographer in front of the San Francisco Opera the night Alberto gave her the record; it was the opening night of the opera and afterwards they spent the night in the Mark Hopkins Hotel. The memories of those magical days over a half-century ago were blurred by the years of summers and winters, blizzards, and smoke from wildfires. Willy had come and gone, her mother and step-father were gone. Annie rarely visited anymore. Snowmelt now dripped into the kitchen through the leaky roof. The boredom of life, the sunrises, and sunsets, hummingbirds, and owls— they all ran together. Opal's hair was snow-white, the mole on her nose was larger and ugly even in her eyes. The attractive young woman Alberto fell in love with was gone.

Holding the remnants of the record, Opal turned toward the view from her front window—the view she used to be able to see from the window. Nowadays, she had to walk outside to see it. The cardboard covering most of the broken windows now hid the magnificent view. Her nieces offered to have the windows repaired, but she always just shook her head and smiled. You get used to something after a while. You even get used to not caring, to giving up.

Summer and the warm Indian autumn were coming to a close. The poplar leaves were turning yellow and the nights were getting chilly. Just the day before she'd heard the first Sandhill cranes flying south. She noticed there was a new pile of firewood stacked outside the cabin. "When did that show up? I don't remember anyone delivering it. Will it be enough for the winter? I'll need coal as well. Coal is much better for heating the cabin."

Sometimes Opal could remember things pretty well, others she drifted in a fog. The past two weeks had been particularly bad. One morning when she tried to get out of bed, she had fallen down. She was dizzy all day and couldn't move her left arm and leg. It got better after a couple of days, but since then, she felt lost much of the time. For awhile, her speech was slurred, but except when her nieces or neighbor Frank Cooper visited, she had no one to talk to except the dogs. Half the time, her talk to the dogs was baby talk anyway, so she didn't know herself how bad it was.

She didn't remember that Frank told her he would come to check on her on cold mornings if he didn't see smoke coming from her chimney. Several times in the past month, he drove down in his battered pickup. She was usually up, shuffling along the rough wooden floor, not really sure what she was supposed to be doing. Frank would knock and wait, the dogs would bark, she would open the door a crack, ask him what he wanted, and he would politely ask how she was. She stared at him for a few seconds, not understanding why he was there. He would ask if she wanted him to start the stove. The first time he asked, she said no, but now she invited him in and let him start the fire. Frank called Terry after the second time this happened. "I'm concerned about your aunt," he told her. "She has a vacant look in her eyes, more so than usual." He didn't tell Terry, but he had been worried about the old lady for a couple of years now; she was getting even stranger. He commented more than once to Alice that he expected he was going to find Opal dead some morning.

Terry called her sisters, and they met one fall evening. Betsy drove down from Glenwood Springs. They understood their eccentric aunt, but they shared Frank's worries. An old woman in her condition could not survive by herself as she had for the past 30 years. Her mind was deteriorating faster. She had no one else to care for her. Or care about her.

They were sitting in Terry's kitchen. After pouring the coffee, Terry looked at Maggie and Betsy and said, "You realize this is her life. She wants to die up there."

Maggie quickly answered back, "Yeah, and she will, sooner than we think. We can't leave her there, but what do we do with her?"

"None of us can take her in," Betsy said. "Terry, Pete would divorce you if you invited her to live here with you." They loved their aunt, but knew that only professionals could deal with her eccentricities. You had to know Opal to love her, but no one except these three and their mother Annie knew her. No one else ever visited Opal, and Opal would rarely have a conversation with anyone else. The only time Opal talked to her neighbors was when they intruded on her with some problem, mostly about her dogs running loose.

Terry ran a finger around the rim of her coffee cup, then looked out the window of her kitchen. "You know it's up to us. She can't make a decision anymore. Things have gotten worse the past year, and especially the last few weeks. She isn't eating properly. I think the dogs would starve if they weren't running all over the country catching whatever they can. I told you last week three of them were shot by neighbors. And Mr. Hunt called this morning to say the old yellow dog got in his chicken house and killed three hens before he shot it. He felt bad, but I agreed he did the right thing."

"We're all thinking the same thing, aren't we?" Betsy asked. She was the least close to Opal, mostly because she lived the furthest away. "Even though I think Opal wants to stay until she drops over dead, I couldn't live with myself if I just let it happen. If I thought she would fall over tomorrow, I would say let her do it. But it won't happen that way and we all know it."

"You remember my neighbor, Mr. Barry?" Terry asked rhetorically. Without waiting for an answer, she continued, "He's the attorney Mother hired to do Aunt Opal's will five years ago. We were talking over the backyard fence the other night. He asked how Opal was doing. Some of Opal's neighbors have talked to him about her." She paused as she got up to refill coffee cups. "I told him about Opal's behavior lately. He laughed and said Opal's behavior has been a subject of discussions many times over the past fifteen years with people who know about her."

"Lord, Terry, Opal has probably been discussed more than anyone in the county for the past 50 years, " Maggie laughed.

"Well, Mr. Barry has only been practicing law here 15 years, otherwise, he would have said 50." All three chuckled. Betsy shifted in her chair.

"Anyway, he said it would be no problem to do the legal work to have her placed in a home. Remember, he did the will several years ago. We are all the family she has left and we can make the decisions. She has no money, but she does have the property."

"Which means she has nothing. That ridge isn't worth anything. Can't farm it, not worth much of anything," Betsy said.

Maggie looked up. "I wouldn't be so sure about that. I had two people in the past year ask me about that place. Said they were interested in buying it. You just wait and see. This valley is going to grow. People are retiring and moving here. This may be a backwater now and certainly no one would want the cabin, but you have to admit, the view is outstanding, even for this country. And it's secluded. Maybe not this year, maybe not five years, but in our lifetime, we may be sitting on a gold mine."

"Well, I wouldn't live up there," Betsy said.

Terry got up again. She seemed restless. "None of us would. But we are close to it—we grew up exploring it. It's isolated, and people are looking for that. But we are straying from the issue." She cleared her throat. "Opal is a danger to herself. We all love her, but we know her days are numbered. She is part of that place. Take her away and she dies. But I can't sleep at night worrying about her. I think of her lying up there starved, or eaten by a mountain lion, or wandering down on the creek, unable to find her way back to the cabin." She looked at Maggie and Betsy, and asked "You can't tell me you don't worry either."

"What do you want to do?" Betsy and Maggie replied in unison.

"We don't have a choice. I can talk to Mr. Barry tomorrow and do whatever paperwork we have to do. I already checked, and the Carriage House in Dawson has openings now. It's not a bad nursing home. She would be taken care of and fed properly. They have a nurse on duty 24 hours a day."

Maggie sighed. "Dammit Terry, you are right and you know it. But we are killing her."

"We are not killing her! We are doing the only sensible thing we can do—we probably should have done this sooner!" Terry pounded her fist on the edge of the table. "It's up to us—since Mother and Dad moved to Colorado Springs. We leave her up there, she will be dead before Christmas."

"We put her in the home, she will still be dead by Christmas," Maggie calmly replied.

"She would rather die up there. You know that," Betsy said as she reached over and put her hand on Terry's arm.

"Yes. And I would rather she did too. But you are not the one that goes up there every other day. You only see her once a week if that often. I can't stand it anymore. I see her wandering aimlessly, half-dressed. I see the filth in the kitchen. I clean the outhouse. You don't deal with that. You can't and neither can Maggie. You both work. I don't. Raising two toddlers is work enough, but I set my own schedule. Winter is coming and she can't light the stove half the days I am up there. It's killing me. I can't deal with it. Are you willing to?" Tears welled in her eyes as her voice cracked.

"She had a long life, " Maggie said. "I won't say a good one. She is a troubled old woman. She was a troubled young lady, but we didn't know her then. We could write a book..." Maggie trailed off as Terry's husband Pete entered the kitchen. He looked at the sisters with their sad and concerned faces. "Jeez, who died? Did I walk into something I don't want to?" Pete put his hands on Terry's back and rubbed it. She reached up and held his hands. "We're talking about Aunt Opal. We all know we are going to have to do something but we don't want to do it."

"Well, speak of the devil," Pete pulled up the fourth chair and sat down, straddling it backward. "Her neighbor Frank Cooper was on the phone just now. He said he saw Opal walking up the lane towards his place an hour ago. He watched her, not knowing what she was doing. She went up to the fence to pet one of his horses standing watching her. She leaned over the fence and fell down. When she got up, her jacket caught on the barbed wire. She struggled awhile and finally she took the jacket off. She fussed with the jacket for a while, then just walked away. She only had a sleeveless undershirt on. You know how cold it is. She walked for a short distance, then fell over. Frank ran across the pasture to her—took him a minute to get there. By the time he reached her, she was sitting swaying back and forth, humming to herself. He said he recognized the tune from one of the opera records. He took her home, wrapping her ripped jacket around her, then came and called me. 'You got one crazy aunt up here. Something has to be done,' Frank said. I agree."

Pete looked at each of the sisters. They all looked at each other, saying nothing. Finally, Terry rose and walked to the phone in the hallway outside the kitchen and dialed a number. After a few moments, she said calmly, "Dick, your neighbor Terry here, 6685. It's Thursday evening. We need to do something with Aunt Opal. It's time. Can we set up an appointment as soon as you have time? Thanks. Talk to you later."

Terry hung up the phone, returned to the kitchen and sat back down. No one said a word. Betsy wiped tears from her eyes. Pete broke the silence. "What is the old saying? You have crossed the Rubicon. You don't have a choice. It has to be done."

The next day, the three sisters met with Dick Barry in his law office in Beaver Creek, then reserved a room at the Carriage House for Opal. Mr. Barry recommended they wait until after Opal was settled in at the Carriage House, then go see Annie and Rand in Colorado Springs where they lived with Annie's brother.

They all agreed it best not to tell Opal ahead of time. They would drive up there—with the sheriff waiting out by the road in case they needed him—and take Opal. She had few possessions; none of her clothes were fit to take with her. They would buy new clothes and would come back later to take care of the dogs and cats, and go through the cabin to see if anything of value remained—including the jars of money in Grandma Della's room that Annie had told them about years ago.

Fourteen

Terry argued with Pete all evening before the 'kidnapping' as
he called it. "Opal deserves to at least say goodbye to her home of over
50 years. It'll be cruel to just take her away. She's as much a part of that
land as the trees and cactus."

"Opal has about as much consciousness anymore as her beloved
claret cup cactus. She has dementia and doesn't even recognize her own
home. Taking her to the nursing home will be quick and is the best
thing to do." That night, Terry hardly slept at all. Neither did Maggie
and Betsy.

When they drove up in Terry's and Maggie's cars—with Sheriff
Hawkins parked out on the road—they found Opal sitting next to the
firewood stacked near the cabin, and cradling a shotgun. The old record
player was playing one of her Puccinis—the needle was caught in a
scratch and the music kept repeating.

Calmly, Opal smiled at them. "Someone is trying to steal my firewood." Terry reached over and gently pulled the shotgun away from
her. She handed it to Maggie, who took it inside, and turned off the
record player.

Terry said gently, "Aunt Opal, we want to take you into town and
buy you a new coat. Will you come with us?"

Opal tried to rock in her chair, then looked down when she didn't
move. "Old rocker must be broke. Won't rock anymore."

Betsy put her hands to her face and quickly turned away. The rocking chair had been broken up and burned for firewood years ago.

Opal smiled and stared at the mountains across the valley. "Can
Willy go with us? Haven't seen him for awhile. He may be down at the
pond. Water hasn't been pumping up here lately." She pointed across
the valley. "If you look closely over there across the Bay, you can see San
Francisco and the opera house where Alberto took me to see my first
opera. I love the ocean. The seagulls are so noisy. I had one land by me
the other day. Have you met Alberto? You will like him. He has been so
nice to me."

"Aunt Opal, let's go into town. Maybe we will meet Alberto. We will leave a note for Willy."

Opal slowly stood up. She started to walk back into the cabin, but Betsy guided her to Maggie's car. Maggie held her breath, but Opal got in the back seat. Terry returned the chair to the porch and looked across the valley. She motioned for the other two to drive Opal off. She would follow in a few minutes.

Terry loved coming here. Clouds were drifting in the bluebird sky. A light dusting of snow from two days ago capped the higher peaks—a sign of the coming winter. A flock of ravens flew from east to west, cawing loudly as they passed over the cabin. They were intent on going somewhere. It was time to change. They lived here, but they had the freedom, and more importantly the motivation to explore.

Watching the ravens disappear, Terry thought about the many times she had seen similar sights of birds. She loved to drive past the adjacent fields and come onto the ridge, with its expansive view of the valley. It was so peaceful. "When was the first time Mother brought us up here? I was a little girl. I remember the lilac bushes, large even then." That's all she remembered from the first few trips. Willy was still alive then, but she couldn't remember what he looked like. One summer day, Opal had been making plum jelly. There were pigs and chickens and a couple of goats wandering around. She helped Opal put the jars of jelly in the root cellar. They had to push the pigs out of the way, then stoop to enter the underground cellar. It had a dirt roof which the goats would lie on; the apricot tree stood right above it. They would nibble on the low branches—Opal throwing rocks at them to get them to move. That was over 30 years ago now.

After Maggie and Betsy drove off with Opal in the back seat and Betsy in the front, Terry walked over to her car and pulled out a new CD player. She set it on the roof of the car and put in the Puccini recording she bought but had yet to give to Opal. She would give it to Opal in her new home. She walked into the cabin and brought out a book she had seen on the kitchen table earlier that week. She held it in her hands, amazed to discover what it was: a large, elaborate King James Bible. Opening it, she read the handwritten inscription on the inside cover: *To Della, on her wedding day, May 14, 1894, from Mother and Father.* Terry had never seen this before. It must have come from the side room that Opal never let anyone into. That was Grandma Della's room when she occasionally stayed with Opal after Thad died. Terry spoke out loud, "This Bible belonged to Opal's mother, given to Grandma by her parents." As far as Terry knew, Opal was not religious and had not even been inside a church in over 70 years. But she had her mother's Bible sitting on the kitchen table, with a large eagle feather marking a page. Why?

Terry opened the Bible at the feather bookmark. It was Ecclesiastes, I-4. The passage was underlined in red ink. She read it out loud. "One generation cometh and another one goeth. But earth abides."

Gently turning pages, she noticed something tucked in further back. She opened it to an old photograph. It was professionally done and showed a smiling young woman, dressed elegantly in a low cut evening gown, fancy earrings, her hair long over her shoulders. Next to her—holding her tightly—was a tall, handsome man, dressed in a tuxedo. "My God, this must be Opal and Alberto. She was beautiful," Terry exclaimed aloud. The couple was standing in front of the San Francisco Opera House and Opal held a thin package tied with lacy ribbon. She turned the photo over. Written on the back were the words, "Opal and Alberto, Love in front of the Opera, the opening of *Turandot*, May 14."

Terry stared at the photo. This was the only picture she had ever seen of a young Opal. And this was Alberto, a handsome man. They both looked so happy. She could feel the emotion, the love captured in this ancient photo. She set the Bible and feather and photo on Opal's porch chair and held her hands to her face, her eyes filling with tears. The photo of the young couple was a window to a magical time.

With Opal's two remaining dogs whining at her feet, Terry stared at the photo for a long time, shocked and heartbroken, unable to move. Terry's thoughts raced through the years and the loneliness of her aunt. She hadn't known Opal when she was young—she only knew the reclusive spinster hermit. But now, seeing this photograph, Terry felt she understood, finally. This was what Opal was running from: she lived a short time in a life of magic but lost it. When she lost the magic, she lost everything worth living for.

After several moments lost in the photograph and lost in time, Terry re-entered the present. Making sure the dogs and cats were outside, she closed the cabin door, replaced the feather and photo in the Bible, and walked slowly over to her car. She laid the Bible on the front passenger seat just as the aria *Nessun Dorma* started playing. She had heard this many times when she visited Opal. It was Opal's favorite. She hadn't known why. Now she did.

The music built to its climax as she stared at the valley below. A breeze wafted a few remaining yellow poplar leaves down onto the car. She looked down the hill at the creek, where cattails rustled in the shifting air currents. She could hear the burble of water flowing over rocks.

A lifelong recluse of this land had just gone; her final chapter near its end. Yet the real life ended decades earlier; the remaining essence of life hung on in sorrow and memories. Here, the forest looked just the same. The birds still flitted in the junipers. The mountains looked as they did when Opal first settled here. The magic still held on for the trees, the birds, the mountains. The land and birds and deer and sky would stay the same. They would not miss Opal, nor even know she had gone. Life would go on. "Earth abides," Terry said, as a magpie landed in the large juniper by Opal's bedroom. It chattered at Terry, then flew on.

Terry let the music play to its end, buoyed by its grandeur. She thought of what it meant to Opal: it let her hold onto the little bit of life in the world out there worth remembering. The rest of it, she let go. Terry wiped her eyes, tears blurring the magnificent view. It was over. Finally. All but the magic—which would live as long as the photo existed.

The second week of December, Opal died in her sleep at the nursing home. She was buried next to her mother, two graves over from Willy, half a continent away from Alberto. On her breast, inside the coffin, lay the photo, her hands clasping it in a grip of love that would last forever.

PHOTO GALLERY

Top: Sunrise from Puccini Ridge.

Bottom: East side of Opal's cabin. Root cellar is between viewer and Della's room. On left, tall matrimony vines among fences.

Top: View of Rock Mesa to the south from near the cabin.
Bottom: Centuries-old juniper tree on Opal's east forty.

Top: Descendents of the magpies that talked to Opal, Terry, and Jake.
Bottom: Typical lichen-covered juniper snag with woodpecker holes.

Clockwise from top left, descendents of the wildlife who shared the homestead: Flip-tail who scolded Opal as she flashed back to her earlier life; Great horned owl who serenaded Opal in her later years; gopher snake Opal saw when she was having her flashback; and cottontails who challenged the dogs and cats, by the rusty barb-wire north fence.

Top: Three-point buck on the trashed hillside east of the cabin. Descendent of the deer that avoided the dogs and nibbled in Opal's garden.
Bottom: One of Willy's old cars still rusting in place 40 years later.

Top: Clouds over Puccini Ridge on a summer day.
Bottom: Opal and Willy's yellow roses around the cabin, 50 years later.

Top: Lilacs that Willy and Opal planted, 55 years later.
Bottom: A descendent of the irises Della shared with Opal, 50 years later.

Clockwise from top left: Sego lily along north fence near Jessie's bridle. Blooming in April or May, depending on spring rains; Claret cup cactus blossoms, one of Opal's favorite flowers on Puccini Ridge; Big prickly pear cactus growing among boulders below Willy's old car.

Top: Bear's cabin 30 years after Opal's death.
Bottom: The final day of Bear's cabin.

Top: View of the much-improved lane 40 years after Opal's death. Looking south toward her gate. Approximately where Thad and Opal met Willy the first time.
Bottom: Sunset from Puccini Ridge.

Part II

Jake's Reflections

THE SPIRIT OF OPAL

Lilacs framing the east view from the cabin.

I was standing by the ancient lilacs, in their spring profusion of purple. They filled the air with fragrance that attracted not only me, but hundreds of sphinx moths as well. The surface of the bushes crawled like moving velvet. I had never seen so many moths. They hovered like helicopters, diving and darting, looking for the perfect blossom—so many to choose from.

There are four huge lilac bushes, each over ten feet tall. I'm sure they are over 50 years old, a remaining grace to a yard that long ago moved past grace into abandonment. I wondered what Opal would think of this place now. She spent years in seclusion in this retreat. What else did she do in the springtime besides tending her lilacs and apricot tree and yellow roses?

Opal Long lived here for probably over 50 years. I don't know exactly. I do know she died in 1988. I read the obituary in the Beaver Creek Museum's files; it didn't say much about her. I have spent hours researching her life, but she left a record nearly as empty as the blue sky on this May evening. She is a mystery and somewhat of a legend on the Mesa. She lived alone in a rotting log cabin for thirty years. She left few heirs and friends. But she left a presence that calls to me just as these lilacs call to the moths.

I 'inherited' the cabin, these lilacs, the owls, deer, pack rats, and the view. Oh, what a view. Sometimes I stare off the edge of the mesa and see what feels like half of Colorado. Opal is as much a part of this place as are the centuries-old junipers, the millennia-old lichens, and the black boulders from distant Grand Mesa to the north. We purchased the property in 1990, only two years after Opal was moved to a nursing home by her relatives. She had to be—she was unable to care for herself any longer. Some say she should have been taken away years before. Her time was up as guardian of this secluded paradise. So she did the only respectable thing she could do. She suffered through nursing home life for a few months, then died. Her body died; her spirit promptly hightailed it back to this place, where it still abides. It lives on in the lilacs and the rabbits, the deer and the claret cup cactus. It sings in the breeze as the wind floats the lilac fragrance past the moths and off into the deepening blue of the Colorado sky. We bought land, built a home, and inherited the spirit of Opal.

I look past the purple of the lilacs, past the sad remains of the cabin, even past the new imposition of our modern home, hanging onto the edge of the mesa which soon drops off into orchards below. My eyes fix on the alpen-glow of the mountains to the southeast. Opal resides there as well. That's what spirits do. They linger on to watch over what they loved and what they lived. She wasn't the first to live here; but she left a mark and she left a mystery. I want to know her, and know that is impossible. She was a widow, a hermit, a recluse, who refused civilization for at least 30 years. She became the lilacs, the cactus, the rocks, the junipers. She guards this view and is somehow trying to instruct me in how to do the same. I don't know if she gave this view—and the feathered and furred animals that roam here—the respect that I do. It doesn't matter. What I don't know about her, I make up. For I believe that spirits can only be good and kind and loving, although sometimes a little mischievous. So the more I learn about her, the less I will have to make up. The moths are telling me that I probably know as much as I will ever find out. Perhaps if I understand the moths I will understand Opal.

I walk back to my new home, thinking about what I will plant in the yard that the deer and rabbits won't eat. She wouldn't have worried much about that; I probably shouldn't either. The deer were here first, even before Opal—much before Opal. One day, my spirit will join hers and we will watch the sunset together as the moths drink their fill of lilac nectar. But until then, I think I will still try to tidy up the place a little. It's the least I can do.

~ J.C. December 1998

THE FREEDOM OF THE BIRDS

123

Bald eagle waiting for Opal's spirit to join him.

As I sat by the abandoned cabin—deserted now for five years—it seemed to be a day of birds. The eagles were soaring and diving in the skies overhead. A magpie talked to me in his indecipherable language as he played hide and seek in the safety of a nearby juniper. Titmice were harassing me for food, this time for a handout of peanuts as I sat on a rock in the warm afternoon sun. It was a day to enjoy the late winter warmth, a preview of warm springtime days soon to come. It was also a time for contemplation on the sky and the birds.

The flight of the eagles overhead in the invisible thermals of warm air was a textbook image of freedom. A display of freedom, but freedom from what? It was freedom to simply play. The only other biological explanation I could think of for this air show was some form of court-ship display. This could very well be since I know that Donna the Great Horned Owl is on her nest now—about fifty yards from the cabin—protected and fed by Fred, her mate. February is early for nesting and egg-laying, but for the big birds, this seems to be a necessity. The sum-mer is short and big birds take a while to grow to self-sufficient size.

Courtship of the eagles, maybe—but to me—it was also something they were doing for the sheer joy of it. They circled higher and higher, becoming smaller and smaller specks of black, finally disappearing in the blue expanse of eternity. Then they fold their wings and free-fall in an explosion of speed, level off, flap their huge wings, and catch another thermal for a soaring, circling rise to do it all again.

I totally lost myself in their displays. I wasn't looking at their color, silhouette, or the identification points listed in bird books. As a matter of fact, I don't know for sure that I may not have been watching falcons instead of eagles. I didn't care. Usually, I pay close attention to details but on this afternoon, I wasn't looking for that. I was part of their flight, enjoying every move they made. They circled into the sun and towards the waxing moon in the eastern sky. They flapped their wings, extended them, and flexed individual feathered fingers, catching every breath of wind. Then, diving, creating a sound of pure excitement as the wind broke in their wake. I sailed with them in their freedom of flight in the ocean of sky.

I also felt a sense of mystery when a magpie came to sit in a juniper as I relaxed near the cabin after lunch. Solitary, away from her usual flock of companions in the open fields, she sat there, hidden from her neighbors, and talked to me. Related to crows and ravens, this large and wonderfully iridescent bird mumbled and chirped and babbled to me in her unknown language. I don't think she even knew I was there and I also don't think she cared if I was. She was expressing herself in the only way she knew. The sounds were a serendipitous symphony. They were loud then quiet, high then low, melodious then grating, changing second-to-second in a non-stop monologue. What was she saying? Was she complaining about her friends and relatives? Or grousing about too little or maybe too much food? Or maybe just expressing her joy to be by herself for a few minutes? The magpie is a social bird, nearly always grouping in flocks of up to a dozen. Maybe they occasionally need to get away, hide in a tree, and just talk. Again, I didn't care about such biological details. She was free and I was free and we just relaxed and connected on some other plane of consciousness on a warm and sunny day.

As I shifted back and forth between work and relaxation on this wonderful winter day, I thought of the birds but also of Opal. I had only begun my research on Opal and knew very little about this former owner of my land. I thought back on how she might have sat on a sunny rock on some long-forgotten February day and watched the birds; that she had long ago forsaken the civilized world of friends and neighbors and had chosen a life of seclusion—had forsaken the freedom these feathery neighbors expressed—her only friends the birds, deer, and other wild critters who shared her spot on earth. She probably didn't care about details of ornithology and whether the finches were House, Cassin's, or Purple. I imagined that she didn't care whether the hawks were red-tailed or Coopers. But she could talk to them and probably did—because she had so few family and friends she really trusted to talk to. Why?

This question haunted me and I couldn't explain why. I had learned she was one of many children. Her father left his family and hightailed it to California to seek his freedom. So Opal became the step-daughter of her mother Della's second husband Thad. Did the loss of her father affect her? Was she angry at God for taking away her father and replacing him with a stranger? She had bad memories of her father, who mistreated and possibly even abused her. Maybe she was relieved. His leaving could have given her a freedom she couldn't handle yet or maybe it deprived her of a freedom she was ready to live.

What I had discovered in my early research was that she had siblings—but was she close to them? Maybe not. She had lots of aunts and uncles, but she was older than her youngest uncle. Della was born in Oklahoma, the oldest of fifteen children. Her grandfather, the first sheriff of neighboring Gunnison County had married a Cherokee in Oklahoma. So Opal had Indian blood in her. Opal's early life was lost to me and there was now no one left alive to ask. I somehow felt disappointed about this. Maybe Opal felt disappointed about something in her early life, too.

Opal moved to California as the wife of a seaman. Her marriage went sour as he treated her badly. He left her with a disease or two, generally unspoken of at the time; and treatments available weren't always effective. It left a terrible gnawing wound that ate at her insides and her mind as well. Maybe that is what embittered Opal to the world. She came back to her old home where she could find the freedom and escape she wanted.

She found her freedom from that world but at the heavy price in freedom of solitude. So she just locked out the world after that and sat alone in her cabin and talked to her birds. She didn't talk to very many people except occasionally at the butt end of her shotgun. She would meet these unwelcome trespassers at her gate. Soon, no one else came by and Opal was left to talk to herself, and the birds.

She lived with dogs and cats in her little log cabin, so I doubt if she spent time watching songbirds. Her cats would have been busy eating them. She also couldn't afford to buy birdseed; in those days, who did? Birds were just like the deer and coyotes. They were there, sharing space with Opal.

But I like to think that occasionally, on a day like today, Opal would walk out of the cabin and sit on a rock in the sun and just stare off into the expansive blue of the Colorado sky. She would gaze on the eagles soaring overhead and listen to the ravens chase after them, scolding and frustrating their big cousins. I imagine she would not always see birds, though—she would see her life as it took a wrong turn somewhere, thinking about why she lost her father, about the evil Mr. Koenig and what he did to her.

Like me, she may have looked over in the cottonwoods in the fields to the east and watched the eagles fly in and out of the trees. One may have been a baldy; others were goldens. No matter. They were big birds and they screamed and squawked in their majestic language as they shifted for position in the tree. One would land, one would take off, seeming to lumber in its slow ascent to the sky, then soar among the clouds. Did Opal realize they had no worries about their past and no delusions about their future? They were free and she was not. She was a prisoner in this secluded paradise of juniper and sagebrush. She was a prisoner as she looked out over a view that symbolized freedom of space and time. A prisoner in my eyes, yet maybe she felt a freedom that many of us do not.

A magpie may have come and sat by her and chirped and mumbled his thoughts. The meadowlark would have sung his cheery song and the chickadees would have scolded everyone in sight. Later, she would have looked overhead as the Sandhill cranes and Canada geese flew in formation towards their freedom to the north. They are part of this place. You cannot separate them from the grass nor clouds or trees. They are all woven together. And Opal was part of it.

Opal loved flowers and grew what she could, sharing with the deer and rabbits. There are still remnants of iris that don't bloom anymore. I bet Opal had a profusion of blooms from them. But like her, they stopped flowering. Some pink flowers remain from an abandoned flowerbed in a little patch of weeds behind the cabin. And of course, the lilacs and yellow roses add grace to what remains of the front and side yards outside the cabin. When Opal watched blooming flowers, she also watched the hummingbirds and butterflies. If she loved the beauty of flowers, she had to love the beauty of the birds as well.

There is a big difference between the flower-birds and the air-birds. The eagles and ravens soar overhead; the hummingbirds and bluebirds keep company closer to earth. But they all have feathers and they sing and chirp and screech their symphony—all seen and heard together, as long as Opal cared to see and to hear. When she could no longer sit on a warm February afternoon and watch the eagles soar over the valley below, she ceased to live at all.

Her time was up and it was a long time she had. She lived for almost eighty-eight years—30 of them by herself in the isolation of her cabin—shared with the eagles. I imagine they understood each other. She had just been waiting until she could fold her wings and dive in the unbridled glee and joy of knowing the sky was hers. Hers to go where she wanted without ghosts of the past holding onto her. Hers to go as a young girl again, free to live a life full of promise that would go right for her. Hers to escape the crowds and fly to a juniper tree and talk to herself, then rejoin her flock. Free to taste the nectar of a lilac and free to fly into the clouds—a freedom we all seek.

I smiled as I watched the black speck of an eagle grow larger as she dove, wings folded toward the green earth. She pulled out in a roar of air and feathers and soared upward again. Thank you, Opal, for that majestic display of freedom. Enjoy the clouds as you disappear into eternity.

~ J.C. 1993

BEAUTY AND UGLINESS

Part of Willy's collection, 50 years later.

For several years, I gave Opal kind words and thoughts, especially as I formulated my vision of her rather sad situation of loneliness and seclusion. Maybe I felt pity for her and thought kindly of her in reaction to that.

Well, let's see the sunlight for what it is: in reality, whatever her state of mind or state of poverty, Opal lived surrounded by filth in this beautiful location. I may later go back to having kinder thoughts about her and how her spirit wafts along in the breeze. Forgive me if I do that; just keep in mind that underneath it all, no matter what I may wish to make her out to be, she lived in filth. Why?

What brought on this change of attitude for me? A shovel, again. I spent an hour or so digging and uprooting the accursed vine that permeates what used to be her yard. This time, it was above the Junkyard Trail, below her cabin. That is what we named the trail that leaves the yard of our new house and wends its way to the upper reaches of what we call Ruby Springs Draw. When we built the trail years ago, we laughed at the rusted cans and old car parts that were strewn along this hillside. From Opal's cabin door, throughout what served as her yard and on down the hill for a good hundred yards: junk. Pure junk. Not future antiques, not a smattering of odds and ends, but a literal dump embedded over two or three acres. Broken glass, bits of baling wire (woven around everything), cans so rusted through they literally fell apart when touched. Bottomless buckets. Bits of metal: on the surface, under the surface, reaching into the sky. A junkyard that we found bothersome, but it seemed to permeate the property. At first, we laughed and spent hours collecting the more aesthetic bits of junk to line the trail with. This was our joke on the situation and we honored this trail with the name Junkyard.

As I sat on a rock on the sunny, warm last day of February, I stopped and thought about the junk: I couldn't dig up or uproot an unwanted bush without getting a shovelful of rusted cans buried in the soil. That day, this junkyard didn't carry the humor we usually saw along the trail. It bothered me. It was an insult to the hillside. It was symbolic of the lifestyle of the hermit and her long-dead common-law husband. It went beyond what could be expected of a dirt-poor pair of recluses living the best they could in poverty. You still don't foul your nest. And that's exactly the conclusion I came to. They did foul this beautiful nest.

Ugliness carries its own definition. I can understand someone living in poverty in a city ghetto. The slum is ugly no matter how you see it; you are surrounded by man-made garbage, with nature eliminated. Nothing man can do to nature in its purity will beautify it; all we can do is uglify it. But when you live surrounded by nature in its unspoiled state, you cannot be allowed to ignore the beauty. The ugliness breaks the sanctity of something rather sacred.

What Opal did was inexcusable. I have thanked her for appreciating beauty since she grew flowers. I praised her for appreciating the birds and animals since she was surrounded by them. Well I was wrong. How can someone understand beauty when you cover it with garbage? How can you love the wild animals when you let your dogs and cats and goats run rampant? Opal was poor and lived in poverty goes the argument. Poor people can light a candle and let it flicker its shadows on a single flower, picked and nestled in a tin can of water. That is understanding of beauty. Beauty from Opal did not cover this hillside. That was sheer ugliness.

Then, I heard the argument Opal had a mental illness. As I would discover in my research on her, that was most likely true. Opal did have problems. To me, that may elicit sympathy and understanding. But on this day, for me, the ugliness overwhelmed everything else.

But, the ugliness was slowly being destroyed by the beauty that cannot be destroyed. I tried to understand in my own mind the difference between beauty and ugliness. I tried to use the senses that Opal had available to her. So, I closed my eyes and listened.

I heard the beauty of the stream below as it splashed in its journey to the sea. The journey of a thousand miles begins just below me where the water surfaces from the depths of the ground as a thousand springs along the hillside. Water which penetrated and seeped, drop by drop, for unknown dozens of feet through sand and gravel and rock underground from who-knows-where to surface into sunlight. Now free again, its drops—as pure as the mountain air—coalesce to form a rushing, happy sound as it falls foot-by-foot on its search for the sea.

I listened again. I heard the soothing background murmur of the wind as it rustled through countless branches and stems of trees and grass. I heard the never-ending serenade of birds as they welcomed the sunlight and pure joy of another day. Spring was coming and they were practicing. All these sounds were beauty brought to life as music.

I closed my eyes again and tried to feel the beauty of the sense of touch. I didn't need to walk around and feel grass and soil and rocks. I just sat there and felt the warmth of the sun enliven my face. Its therapeutic warmth made me feel alive and welcome on this hillside. The breeze caressed my skin like a massage.

Opening my eyes, I looked for the beauty. It was easy to see. As I scanned the horizon, I saw in every direction the panorama of snow-covered peaks and gentle valleys of the Colorado Rockies. I saw the clouds paint the blue of the sky with wisps and swirls. I once answered a question of what was my favorite color with the following: my favorite color is the blue of a Western sky right where it meets the pure white of a puffy cloud. Not the color blue, not the non-color white, but the contact where the white makes the blue explode in intensity. I could add to that today by saying the blue of the sky where it meets the green of the cedar tops is another favorite color. When I got tired of looking at the distance, I looked at my feet. The colors of the lichens on the black boulders countered the dull tans and yellows of dried grass. The grays of the juniper trunks countered the olive yellow-green of the needles. The juniper berries were scattered throughout the green as if sprayed by a paint can. Color, form, texture, the placement—all this defined beauty just as the junk defined ugly. But the beauty was slowly hiding the ugly as will always happen, given time.

Surely Opal was able to hear, feel and see the beauty I saw today. This is not a city slum with man-made ugliness. This is a living breathing explosion of beauty regardless of how poor you are. It makes one think about how poverty can sometimes be a state of mind, no matter how difficult it is to survive day-to-day.

In talking to Opal's former neighbors, they described her variously as unkempt, snaggletooth, a witch, and the goat lady. All stereo-typical descriptions of ugliness. She lived amid beauty in her own ugliness. She let the dogs sleep under the covers. Her cats took over in her final days. Her cabin—her hovel—became so fouled that she was afraid to light the woodstove on a cold morning for fear that it would ignite the built-up cat litter piled inches deep under the stove. And the saddest part of all this was the fact she was a pretty young lady. She gave up. On herself and her life.

I understand that pioneers often made their own dumps. I understand throwing things in a pile, even close to a cabin. Archeologists (amateur and professional) search through those dumps nowadays seeking purple bottles and other artifacts. A midden is one thing. A midden of three acres attributed to only two people is another. It is not just a matter of slovenliness. This type of disregard for any type of cleanliness is an indication to me of lack of respect for oneself. This comes back to my feelings of sadness and forgiveness for Opal. She was a lonely woman, more importantly, a frightened woman. Her only contact with a world that terrified her died when Willy fell over one day clutching his chest. He was dead in seconds. Opal screwed up every ounce of courage in her body and walked up to her neighbor's house. Neighbors she had never met. She had never met nearly all her neighbors for decades. She knocked on the door and asked for help. The neighbors had never met Opal and would not meet her again in the next ten years, although they lived within a quarter-mile of her. Opal buried Willy and lost whatever respect she still had for the outside world and for herself. She also lost whatever respect and appreciation she had for the beauty she lived amidst.

So, I lost a bit of my respect for Opal as I sat on the rock just above the Junkyard Trail. I knew I would continue to analyze her as I cleaned and sorted and re-stored the beauty of this ridge. I would remove the rusted cans and broken glass, uproot the accursed vines as they puncture me, and challenge my definition of what belongs here. They don't belong. Not because they have thorns and form impenetrable thickets, but because they aren't native and that is my primary definition of what should be here and what should not. I admit my definition is daily shattered by my own hand as I plant apple trees and butterfly bushes. But get beyond my yard and my garden, I define acceptable as what belongs here naturally. I can even accept that an Opal could be natural, but only if she acted with some respect for what was here. She didn't in my judgment. And I cannot forgive her for that.

But—as I analyze her, and even once glorified her innocence—I am now erasing her. I am carting her off to the dump as I carry off the rusted cans and tangled fence wire. I watch her memory go up in smoke as I burn the old boards and dried vines.

Naively, I thought I was being thanked by the juniper and the lichen-covered rocks, the pack rats and the Great Horned owls, as I cleaned up this place. "Well thank you very much," I could hear the breeze murmur, "but we are doing quite well on our own. We do not need your help." Beauty, just like ugliness, carries its own definition and that is spelled apathy. Nature doesn't care. It is beauty by definition and it will reclaim everything. There may be rusted cans and broken bottles that cover this hillside. Opal may have not cared or Opal may have cried as she saw what she did. Either way, it is unimportant to the juniper and lichen-covered rocks. Give it a year, give it a thousand. At some time, it won't matter. I will be long gone, just like Opal, when at some point, the rock will be here, as will the distant mountains, a few wispy clouds, and a spray-painting of bluish berries on green juniper needles that blend with a blue sky and white clouds. The birds will sing and the world will be beautiful. And deep below the soil on this hillside, there will be trickles of spring water that surface and start a long journey to a sea. A sea that rearranges whatever falls into it from sky or shoreline or river estuary and creates beauty. Even beauty of some far-off mountain-top where people used to live.

~ J.C. 1998

OF BRAMBLES AND OLD FENCES

The window-window on the
front porch of the cabin.

It was a sunny January day and for the last month, I had been cooped up for too many cloudy, cold, and snowy winter days in my new home. I stood outside, breathing in the warmth of the intense blue sky, trying to decide what to do next. There was so much. I had brush to uproot, tin cans to dig out of the frozen soil, and the cabin to clean out.

The cabin—the multi-year project—beckoned me. The cabin was a magnet that pulled at me. It was Opal and Willy, the remains of their life. There was not much else left of them. There were a few old car parts that Willy had dragged onto the place and scavenged for something usable, something worth a dollar. Wood-burning cook stoves, barrels, buckets, and junk still dotted the hillside. Everything he thought was worth anything, he brought here. And it lay scattered amongst the sagebrush and juniper, rusting and rotting. The pack rats that filled the cabin with their distinctive odor—the repulsive and disgusting smell that surrounds you as you near the cabin—have nothing on Willy. He was the ultimate pack rat.

Now, the cabin—where he and Opal spent long January nights huddled by the woodstove—sat here like a giant rat midden. Since it was hard to even approach the building, overgrown and protected by brambles, I decided to start cleaning up the yard, or what was left of a yard. It was filled with the obnoxious thorny bush that had taken over the yard and surrounding hillside. I tried to identify it. One person called it a matrimony vine and another said goji berry. It is a nightshade, with distinctive purple and yellow flowers. The other brambles intermixed with the vine were yellow roses—long gone wild and unruly.

Maybe at one time Opal had planted the obnoxious purple-flowered vine as a hedge, or maybe it just appeared. However it got here, and whatever it is, it went wild, taking over with its expanding root system and sharp thorns. I've dug and pulled and uprooted off-and-on for several years. It only seems to be invigorated by this jostling of its roots. It comes up again in force, but smaller. Maybe by attrition, I could wear it down. That is if I didn't wear down my fingers and legs from the thorns; it is tough on gloves. The thorns always seem to find the holes in my gloves. And my gloves always seemed to have holes, no matter how new they were. But this is a war and I am determined to win. Until I do, the going is tough.

The problem with the yard when I began was that the vines had grown up and around and into old chicken wire and woven wire fences that used to delineate something. They may have kept in—or out—the chickens or pigs or sheep or other menagerie that kept Opal and Willy in some type of food. The fences are only kept standing now by the vines, and to take out one, I have to take out both. Anyone who has ever had to pull out bindweed or other spreading vines from a fence can understand this struggle. But it was a magnitude or two worse with these, since they not only have thorns, they grew over the years up to ten feet tall, with woody stems two-to-three inches in diameter. If I uprooted them, which I had to do, then I spent hours unweaving the branches from the wire. I came to hate chicken wire. In a way, I admired these ancient plants since most of the older stems were covered with lichens and moss. Beauty covering ugliness and despair. There may be some hidden meaning of life in that one.

I had to stop and chuckle on occasion, thinking of Opal so proudly assembling her fences out of whatever scraps of barbed wire, wood, posts, sheep fencing, and baling wire she had on hand (probably from Willy's wire and scrap lumber piles). She built a fence, and no doubt it worked for whatever purpose she had in mind. But now the half-buried rotting bottom boards, wired onto the rusted and mangled chicken wire fencing—held together by these cursed vines—somehow had an obstinacy that I had to respect. They brought to life the stubbornness of Opal that I could only imagine as she cheerfully whistled while she wired the fence together on some forgotten October afternoon decades ago.

As I was taking a break, I stood by the front of the cabin. My pulling of vines revealed details of a front window that had been hidden for at least a decade by the tangled mass of vining branches. This window was not your normal window, but two old Model-something-or-other vintage car or truck windows, held in place by very large bent nails (rusty of course). What a find! Most of the windows in the cabin had long fallen out, with broken glass lying on the ground and window frames hanging in various stages of rot or disarray. This window was Opal and maybe Willy at their best: they had used some of Willy's car parts as a source, quite ingenious actually, for a window. And I imagine quite valuable in today's antique-crazed society.

How long had this treasure of a window been hidden in the southeast corner wall of the porch? Ten years? Twenty? Probably more since Opal has been dead for ten years. And Willy for over 40. I thought back to when this innovation was new. Did Willy install it, or did Opal make do in those 30 years she survived in this place by herself? I know she had to be resourceful; just look around at the cabin. The walls papered with old newspapers held into place with canning jar lids nailed on the wall. I was struck by the "Vote for Ike and Dick" full-page newspaper ad of 1952. Or was it 1956? Willy was alive then. They might have sat in the cabin at night discussing the qualities of Eisenhower versus Stevenson after enjoying a supper of home-canned potatoes, pork chops, and apricot pie, all raised from their garden and home butchering.

After I discovered the car-window window, I found myself just standing there talking to the cabin. What did go on in this dilapidated ruin of a home? Opal lived here for such a long time after Willy fell over dead. He had a varied and interesting life, was a jack of all trades, and obviously a scrounger. I didn't think of him very often. I thought of Opal. I could look in the cabin and see her sitting alone by the woodstove. I saw her watching TV, however limited or poor her reception probably was. I saw her tending her cats and dogs and living with (or maybe trying to forget) her memories. She rarely left the property and became more and more solitary. This cabin and immediate surroundings were her life.

I stepped closer and looked inside at the mess. Rags and old beaten-down cardboard boxes littered the floor. The newspaper wallpaper was in tatters. The roof leaked, but this didn't matter since the windows were mostly gone. There were two refrigerators, covered with streaked rat- and who-knows-what-else droppings. This remnant of a person's life was in total disarray and filth. In her prime, would Opal have been bothered by what had happened to her home? I had no idea.

I could have rambled on in my mind as I stared into the front porch with its old mattress and rusting bedsprings. As in any old building, what is left in tattered ruins can only hint at the former inhabitants. The matrimony vine—and cheatgrass—steadily but solidly reclaimed this home. The pack rats and weasels, ground squirrels and mice called this home. No telephone to interrupt the February night's silence; no glare of TV with Lawrence Welk dancing amid the champagne bubbles. Only the ghost of an old woman sharing the silence with her memories.

Loneliness shouted back at me as I dug and yanked at the vines creeping up through the logs and boards of the front porch walls. I tore the rolled asphalt siding off, exposing the brown and orange weathering of old wood planks. Some of the long-exposed boards were now brightly covered with green and red and orange lichens, matching that on the oldest of the matrimony vines. I crunched rusted cans as I walked. They—and old light bulbs, bottles, and assorted other garbage—were half-buried in the yard. Time was eating away at the cabin, but my impatience would not allow it to continue much longer. Slowly, but more quickly than the natural process, I was removing the story of this woman and her long-dead companion.

As I uncovered an old pitchfork, lying entangled in vines and grass, I imagined the last time it was used. The handle was almost rotted off but somehow held together by colorful lichens. As I dug into the rock border next to the porch, which once held iris or daisy or other colorful flowerbeds, I uncovered an old pick. It was almost entirely buried and the handle held onto the rusted metal by only a fiber. Then an old hoe. I imagined a day long ago as Willy set this pick against the side of the cabin: he had been digging in the backyard, working on the old cistern. The ground was unmercifully rocky and he needed the pick. He laid it aside as he stopped for an afternoon lemonade and may never have touched it again. Opal probably used the hoe to hack weeds out of her potatoes and beans. She may also have used the pitchfork to throw hay to the milk cow; it was set against the fence and remained there after the old cow died and Opal could never again afford to buy a new source of milk. The abundance of condensed milk tins near the cabin traced the slowly receding distance of her garbage from the cabin. In her last days, living on condensed milk, she barely threw things out the door, much less far down the hill. Did the pitchfork sit there until a strong storm one May afternoon blew it over, never to see the sun again until this January afternoon?

What stories did the old gutter have, now swinging in the wind, hanging by only a strand of rusted baling wire? The old stock tank rusted through, next to the row of crumbling truck tires? The pieces of white sheets of an old metal shed, obscured by cheatgrass? The two squares of rusted wire window screen, crumpled underneath a pile of bottles?

I had spent the day in the front yard. There was still a day's work left here, just clearing it enough to be able to walk through. I left the sides and back for another day, another week, another year. There was still the root cellar, earth roof caving in, log beams cracking and sagging onto the rows of jars and bottles. There was still the unknown mess lying next to the side room, hiding who knows what? And of course, there was the inside of the cabin, waiting for a good mask to protect me from unknown and dangerous microbes and viruses and other poisons from the layers of filth. That was all to wait until a much later day.

In my uprooting, I found a small round metal tag that solved one mystery for me. It identified a multiflora rose, patented as *Sonia*. How old was this? After minor pruning of dead branches earlier last spring, we were treated to a blast of yellow from the clump and tangle of what we had thought were wild rose bushes. Untamed now, but planted one spring by Opal. *Sonia*—maybe a new variety of beautiful yellow rose at the time. In the six years we owned this property before finally moving here, we had never seen the roses bloom: here was hidden beauty, just waiting for me and a wet autumn a year ago. They joined the four ancient giant lilac bushes in glorious color explosions this spring. I thought of Opal and thanked her. Some beauty did come through from her. I have to think in her heart she was a woman who appreciated beauty. I don't know, and never will. But by living here, she was exposed to beauty every day whether or not she understood it.

I like order and will restore my version of it here. One day it will be gone, as will be the memories of Opal. I will try to learn about her life and capture her memories. It will be difficult, as much as trying to restore natural order to this bramble of vines and cheatgrass. I peeled away memories as I uprooted vines and tore down boards. The flames and smoke from the piles of boards and brush will eventually send all memories floating on the wind. Then there will be simply the chattering of the titmice and the fleeting shadow of an eagle, riding the wind of his kingdom. There will be only the sound of the wind as the clouds float by on sunny January afternoons far in the future.

~ J.C. 1999

Root Cellar

Yard of the cabin looking at root cellar entrance, during excavation.

I felt guilty as I stood looking down into the root cellar, another part of Opal's legacy. I had spent days clearing junk from the area around the cellar, which I had to do first to be able to even get to the cellar roof. Then I shoveled a ton or more of soil, coal ashes, and small rocks off the roof. This also made me feel guilty since deer had periodically used this soft soil as a bed.

No longer. The soil was piled around the cellar where junk used to be; the pieces of corrugated metal strips, metal car parts, and pieces of cardboard that served as the final sheathing to hold the soil, rocks and ashes, were stacked in separate piles of burnable and non-burnable. Then the boards, slabs of logs, and finally, logs, had come off. Sunlight on this bright spring morning shone into the formerly dank and dark cellar, light touching jars and bottles for the first time in decades. Opal's secrets and parts of her private life now lay exposed.

I knew that things lay hidden in this root cellar. Parts of the roof and sides had long ago caved in and I had been told that she had old brass lanterns and other valuable things that were long ago abandoned when the small cave-ins had started. The damage was evident. Soil covered everything and some shelves were totally buried. I surveyed the remnants of this once usable cellar as I shuddered with dismay at the task of digging through it all. I had done the preliminary work to get to the archeological site. Now the real work of discovery lay before me.

But why did I feel guilty? I was standing outside looking in a window of Opal's life like a peeping tom. She would never have allowed me to get this close. Digging through her cellar was invading private secrets of her life. I would see what she ate, what she saved, what she stored, in this, the final bank vault of her life's possessions.

Stepping carefully over the pile of metal and wood that was the result of the unroofing, I stopped and looked around me. The cellar was in what would have been the side yard of the old cabin, whose east wall was only a few dozen inches away. I was right outside the window, next to her bedroom as I worked. I felt her spirit watching, unable to do anything to stop me.

I chuckled as I thought of Willy carefully raiding his own auto graveyard to find pieces of car doors and folding hood covers from vehicles that I probably have never heard of. He laid these, interwoven with corrugated sheets of metal to cover the board slabs that he undoubtedly picked through from an abandoned sawmill. Some of the metal was rusted into shreds, while other pieces were remarkably whole. Everything was now bound for the dump.

As I gazed down on the few jars exposed within the top layer of earth, I spotted a Ball Mason jar that didn't look right. I cautiously stepped down into the cellar for my preview search and picked up the jar. It was a half gallon-sized jar. I had never seen such a thing before. I carefully picked it up and carried it outside, my first prize discovery. What more lay hidden in this dusty jumble?

I had to duck as I worked the north end. The old apricot tree, leaning perilously to the east and somehow still alive, was hanging low over the cellar roof. The tree was half dead, but new buds were just days away from covering the tree with pink and white blossoms. This tree, probably a product of a seed spit out by Willy as he lazed outside on an early summer afternoon, had weathered the history I longed to discover. It guarded the root cellar and added color for well over half a century. It now clung to survival, hidden by brambles and yellow roses. Around its base were scattered more piles of old pipe, rusted metal, broken jars, chicken wire.

Standing here on this spring morning, with apricots ready to blossom, cheat grass greening up, bluebirds and wrens singing arias to the sky, I did see the beauty that Opal would have seen. Surely, she did keep the weeds out of her yard. Surely, she could walk around the cabin without struggling through the brambles and tripping over junk. I had to think that. I had to believe that only in her final years did she succumb to sloth. Time has a way of making it difficult or impossible to do the physical work required to keep a place up—adding to apathy or maybe just trying to cover it up.

I tried to picture Opal walking out on a day like this to get a jar of apricot jam, stored neatly on the shelf of her food vault. She would have paused to listen to the wren warbling his heart out. She would have seen the iris breaking green into the sunlight. She would have seen the ermine, now mottled brown and white as he scurried under the outhouse. She would have felt the breeze as it blew warmth in from the south, just ahead of the March streaks of clouds that just might bring a few drops of rain down here, snow flurries higher up.

Only towards the end, I imagine, did she fill cardboard boxes with every jar she emptied. I have seen this evidence already, as I noticed the few jars and bottles sticking up out of the earth—the flotsam bobbing on the surface of the dusty, rubble sea. But then, as evidenced by the hillside garbage dump, it did seem like she saved everything she ever purchased or borrowed. This was a person who was on the edge of survival most of her life. She was a child of want, a refugee of the Depression, victim of hard times, a recluse who shunned civilization. Maybe she did save everything. All the things that deserved better than the hillside dump went into the root cellar.

Carefully sifting through decades of accumulation, I would still not find out who she really was. Were the whiskey and wine bottles hers or Willy's? Did she can her food, or did her mother or other relatives do it for her? Would I find the old brass lanterns, or was that a myth told to add to her mystery? Was it another myth that she hid what little money she had in a jar, either buried in the root cellar or buried in a hole in the ground, to forever lie in wait of discovery?

I looked down into the newly exposed rubble of the cellar and then turned to look at the cabin. I apologized to Opal as I felt her spirit watching me. I had dismantled her privacy as surely as I had removed her cellar roof. I didn't think I'd ever get her to understand; I'm not sure I'll ever understand. I had to search, just as the wren had to sing and the *Sonia* roses had to leaf out on a late March day under a sunny sky with a hint of rain off in the distance.

Taking a deep breath, and crouching low, I ducked into the cellar. Shafts of light filtered through the apricot tree above, to the shelves, half-covered in soil, through the exposed glass of jars and bottles. Dust motes filled the air. I knew what I would find and very little of it would be worth saving. As I carefully lifted jars, soil and pebbles jostled to fill in gaps on the shelves. More soil sifted down from the sides of the cellar, once again covering a good Mason jar, dozens of old empty ketchup bottles, broken jars, metal canning jar lids, broken slabs of wood.

I had to surface every few minutes to get a breath of fresh air. As I poked my head up, a big-eyed doe wandered by, looked at me, and bounded away from the strange-looking badger that had popped up out of this hole. I glanced again at the far-off mountains, still capped with a snowy cover. I looked again at the piles of trash surrounding the cellar. I knew this may be a fruitless effort, but I had to do it. The spirit of Opal urged me on, at the same time cursing my presence. It would be a slow process, but I had the time. Time was about all I would find, time that hid years of loneliness, seclusion, secrets of a reclusive woman.

~ J.C. 2001

The Bridle

Jessie's bridle, 33 years after Opal's death.

THE BRIDLE AND BIT are hanging on a small branch of a small juniper tree near the north border of the property. We had not seen it in our 30 years of wandering the 40 acres, exploring virtually every square foot—or so it seemed. This had escaped our notice.

The leather is weathered—with lichens on the surface—but still intact. The bit is solid, although showing signs of rust and weathering. The reins have braided leather sections, obviously made with care and patience. The reins hang nearly to the ground and have not been chewed by mice or other leather-loving animals. The juniper is less than twenty feet tall, and less than ten inches in diameter. But it has to be well over thirty years old, unlike some of the nearby trees measuring into centuries.

"Who placed it here and why? And what is its story?" I looked into the sky and asked the spirit of the rough-legged hawk circling above. I knew the hawk had to have some contact with Opal—the previous guardian and inhabitant of this land for over half a century. The hawk told me the following story.

The bridle was made by a young Arapaho girl well over a century ago. She had obtained the leather straps and metal parts when her small band ambushed a group of white settlers who had raided her camp and killed her family. She repaired it and braided the reins, as her father had taught her. Her people normally used rope without the bit; they felt that the bit degraded the horse since it meant they had control over the animal. They felt equal to the animal, as they did with all creatures. They would use their spirit guides to coax their equal partner—the horse—to move the way they wished. In this case, she felt it necessary to make this one special. Her new horse, once belonging to her brother, became sacred to her. When she became the wife of a Ute warrior who visited her camp, she, the bridle and reins went west to the other side of the great mountains. That life soon ended when the Ute were rounded up and forced to leave their homeland and settle on a reservation far away. In the confusion of this move, her horse with bridle was claimed by white settlers in this valley.

When the horse died of old age, Whitney—a later farmer in the area—found the bridle in a field where the horse died. He admired the workmanship and polished the leather and bit until it sparkled like new. He used the bridle on his mule, which he occasionally rode into town, but mostly used her to plow his fields of corn and wheat. Whitney's daughter Opal would ride the mule to school during the winter. Opal didn't like the names Jennie and Jack often used for mules, so she named the young mule Jessie. After Whitney deserted Opal and the rest of his family to move to California, Opal's mother Della married Thad, who loved the mule.

After many years, Jessie became old and nearly blind. Thad didn't use her anymore and said he was going to have to dispose of her. Opal had recently returned after several years in California, and had obtained eighty acres on a nearby mesa through the Homestead Act. She had been emotionally wounded and desired a place to get away from the world that had abused her. Although Opal seemed unable to love or care for any other person, she could not stand to see Jessie put down. When she learned Thad's intentions, she begged her mother and step-father to let her have Jessie. She would let her roam her sagebrush and juniper land and live out what remained of her days.

There was little feed for even an old mule, but Opal and her partner Willy made sure she was fed like a queen. Willy, who was known to have sticky fingers and often showed up with all kinds of useful things, actually worked odd jobs at the local feed store to buy a sack of oats once a week. In a ritual going back to her childhood, Opal would put the bridle on Jessie and lead her around, talking sweet nothings in her ears. Jessie would nuzzle Opal and snort her version of thank you.

Although Opal showed little emotion or care for most people, she cared deeply for Jessie. When she went out to feed oats to Jessie one December morning, she found the mule lying dead by the north fence line. She and Willy labored all day to dig a grave in the almost frozen ground and push Jessie into it. As she hung the bridle on an inside wall of her cabin, she renewed her vow that no one would ever put a bit in her mouth; she would do what she wanted, with no control over her by anyone. The bridle stayed there for decades, protected from the weather.

Years after Willy died, and Opal had deteriorated in old age, she went out one early spring morning to Jessie's grave. She ducked under the low branches of a small juniper tree, which she felt served as a proper grave marker, and hung the bridle on a branch. She caressed the bit and braided reins, then turned and slowly walked back to her cabin. She vowed once again to the mule that neither of them would ever have a bit forced in their mouths. Opal was soon taken away from her home and refuge and died within months in a nursing home.

I touched the bridle and thought of its long history. I debated taking it down and hanging it on the wall of one of my buildings but decided that it should stay where Opal last put it. The bridle, the forgotten grave of a long-dead mule, and the memory of a young Arapaho girl and her horse, as well as the legacy of Opal, will remain as long as the hawk soars overhead in a brilliant blue sky and the nearby claret cup cactus blooms on warm spring days.

~ J.C. 2021

Freeing of the Soul

Site of Bear's cabin, and the ancient juniper as grave marker for both cabins.

On a January day in 2003, Amos unloaded and drove his excavator up to Opal's old cabin and tore it to shreds. It had stood for more than half a century, falling more and more into disrepair. Since I bought the property, I had been cleaning up the junk in the area surrounding the cabin and down the hill to the creek. Now the cabin itself was the last remaining obstacle to our own plans on the main ridge. It was time for it to go. Dust flew, pack rats scurried to safety, and logs, boards, and windows were piled into a mound, twice as high as my head. The old cabin—where Opal and Willy spent thousands of winter nights in front of a wood stove—was now a heap of trash. Amos loaded his big machine on his truck and drove off. I lit a match and sent dark smoke into the otherwise blue skies. Along with the smoke drifted the spirit of Opal.

The fire burned for three days. After the ashes cooled, Amos returned to load the ash and metal into his dump truck, drove over to the west cabin, and buried the remains nearby. I spent hours raking the empty spot where the cabin once stood, then piled the foundation stones between two of Opal's lilac bushes. All evidence was soon gone, other than bare earth. The smoke would circle the Earth as molecules of carbon and nitrogen. I wondered if Opal would enjoy the trip. Surely, I thought, she was watching somehow. What did she think of me and my destruction? Did this help free her? In my vision, she was young and pretty and full of hope.

On a late March day, 2021—with threatening clouds darkening the northern horizon—Amos returned, drove his excavator up to the west cabin, and dug a big hole: a grave of sorts. His mechanical dinosaur tore the old building to shreds—in a sight reminiscent of the scene eighteen years earlier—and buried the remains in the new grave, just a few short yards from the earlier burial. This was the last building that Opal would have known. She didn't live in it and no one alive now really knows the full story of that building. But now that was history. Gone forever.

After Amos drove away, I walked to the now-empty site, covered with fresh earth and rocks. I knew that this was the last major thread to be broken. Opal was now totally free. Her spirit released, this time in full, to roam the distant skies. I thought back to my full-circle feelings for Opal. At first, I honored her spirit—a spirit that escaped a life unkind to her and found refuge here. Then I cursed the old woman who fouled her nest, strewing garbage over a once beautiful landscape. Now, as I knew the full story or as much as anyone will ever know, I felt the sorrow and sympathy this damaged woman deserved. Her bones, and those of her strange partner Willy, rest in a cemetery seven miles distant, in unmarked paupers' graves. But their spirits had been detached from the bones and hung around her place of refuge, tied by invisible thread. Now, the bones of two old cabins lie buried in peace. A majestic centuries-old juniper—which had shaded the west cabin—stands sentinel, a proper grave marker.

I imagined Opal's spirit drifting away in the springtime breeze, white-topped mountains lining the far horizon. A hermit found safety and solitude in this refuge, escaping from the evils of the world she had withdrawn from. No one would ever know the demons that ate on her very soul. I'll never know what I helped destroy. It is over; she is gone, now at peace.

I looked into the skies to see if I could see her spirit flying free. I spotted two eagles so high they were barely dots in an infinite sea of blue. Yes, that was Opal. She found Alberto and he was waiting for her. They disappeared as they flew over the nearby mountains. This was the freedom Opal had searched for. She had been locked onto Earth in her place of refuge, seeking those high snow-capped peaks which signified a freedom unavailable to her for so long. Alberto was the only person who had ever really loved her. She held onto it for decades, in lonely isolation.

I also knew that deep down, I myself had been searching for some closure to my exposure to Opal. She had affected me as well, by my confusion about this damaged woman. She had suffered abuse in her bright and promising youth. A young woman who escaped and sought refuge from the world she was trapped in. Now that she is free, maybe I will be free as well.

I looked at the stately juniper standing guard over the two buried buildings. This tree symbolizes what was here all along. The beauty of the spring blooms of the sego lilies and claret cup cactus, the grace of the gnarled and twisted ancient junipers, the spring migrations of Sandhill cranes flying far overhead, the antics of the chipmunks and pack rats. They all belong. This is their home and always will be. This is forever and we all are passing guests.

I looked up at the sky once again as a raven flew by and disappeared to the west. I watched cumulus clouds drift from the north, the earlier dark threat of rain now gone. I felt a drop on my hand. I tried to focus but I couldn't clear my eyes. I bowed my head to say goodbye to all the spirits now freed. It was turning out to be a beautiful spring day after all.

~ J.C. 2021

Acknowledgements

There are many people I need to thank for the help they gave me. They fall into two groups: those I interviewed to find out the story of 'Opal' and 'Bean Ridge'; and those who reviewed and commented on the *Hermit of Puccini Ridge*.

After my wife and I purchased the property that once belonged to Opal, I interviewed as many 'old-timers' as I could find who may have known her. They were mostly neighbors, a few relatives, and others who lived in the area at that time (1930-1988). All were very helpful and most consented to taped oral interviews, which I donated to the Hotch-kiss-Crawford Historical Society for their oral history records. Nearly everyone stated they didn't know Opal very well, or only by reputation; hardly anyone really knew the reclusive old lady.

I talked with: Edith Watson, Dorothy Ware, Nelda Widener, Willy Manz, Stan and Edna Purnell, Earl Hildebrand, Betty Kuta, Barb Phillips, Jim Edwards, Glen Watson, Leroy and June Reed, Ward Holder, Wayne 'Squash' Wise, Marie Reed, Don Short, Emily McAllister. Sadly many of these people have now passed.

When I became immersed in writing her story, I asked several people to be readers for me. This was a new experience for me. I wish to thank Anne Ferguson Monahan, Bill Englehardt, Marie Brookhart, Lynn deBeauclair, Erica Steiner, and Sharyl Peterson.

Special thanks to Connie King for her amazing talents at book design—so much more than cover-to-cover.

The book would not have been possible without the astute editing of my wife Katherine Colwell.

Joseph and one of many massive ancient junipers
he is inspired by every day. Opal called these
centuries-old junipers, 'grandfather' trees.

About the Author

As a second career, Joseph Colwell has authored seven books—three nature-related essay collections; a novel; a memoir; the novella and short story collection *Tales of Ravens Nest*; and now *The Hermit of Puccini Ridge*. *Hermit* is the first book of his "Ravens Nest" trilogy—the prequel to *Tales of Ravens Nest*. Book three is waiting in the wings.

Although he grew up in a small Illinois town, Joseph has spent over 50 years living and working across the West. During his college years at the University of Idaho studying forestry and wildlife management, he worked in Idaho State Parks, and Mt. Rainier and Grand Canyon National Parks. He then spent over 27 years with the US Forest Service in five different national forests in four states. After retirement from the Forest Service, he spent ten summers doing fire information work on wildland fires, assisting the media and homeowners in understanding wildfires.

Joseph and his artist wife Katherine live and work on their 40-acre nature preserve in western Colorado. They specialize in assisting others in exploring creativity, using nature as the source of inspiration. They can be reached at ColwellCedars.com.

www.ingramcontent.com/pod-product-compliance
Lightning Source LLC
Chambersburg PA
CBHW061103100726
47911CB00012B/358